B. B. KING

Joe Nazel

MELROSE SQUARE PUBLISHING COMPANY
LOS ANGELES, CALIFORNIA

Joe Nazel is America's most prolific African American writer, having published forty-six fiction and non-fiction works. Educated in ethnic studies at the University of Southern California, he teaches and writes in Los Angeles, California. For the Black American Series, he is the author of biographies of Martin Luther King, Jr., Langston Hughes, Thurgood Marshall, Ida B. Wells, as well as B. B. King.

Cover Painting by Jesse Santos
Cover Design by Jesse Dena.

B. B. KING

MELROSE SQUARE BLACK AMERICAN SERIES

ELLA FITZGERALD
singer

NAT TURNER
slave revolt leader

PAUL ROBESON
singer and actor

JACKIE ROBINSON
baseball great

LOUIS ARMSTRONG
musician

SCOTT JOPLIN
composer

MATTHEW HENSON
explorer

MALCOLM X
militant black leader

CHESTER HIMES
author

SOJOURNER TRUTH
antislavery activist

BILLIE HOLIDAY
singer

RICHARD WRIGHT
writer

ALTHEA GIBSON
tennis champion

JAMES BALDWIN
author

JESSE OWENS
olympics star

MARCUS GARVEY
black nationalist leader

SIDNEY POITIER
actor

WILMA RUDOLPH
track star

MUHAMMAD ALI
boxing champion

FREDERICK DOUGLASS
patriot & activist

MARTIN LUTHER KING, JR.
civil rights leader

ZORA NEALE HURSTON
author

SARAH VAUGHAN
singer

LANGSTON HUGHES
poet

JAMES BECKWOURTH
mountain man

PAUL LAURENCE DUNBAR
poet

ALVIN AILEY
dancer/diector

HARRY BELAFONTE
singer & actor

JOE LOUIS
boxing champion

MAHALIA JACKSON
gospel singer

BOOKER T. WASHINGTON
educator

NAT KING COLE
singer & pianist

GEORGE W. CARVER
scientist & educator

WILLIE MAYS
baseball player

LENA HORNE
singer & actress

DUKE ELLINGTON
jazz musician

BARBARA JORDAN
congresswoman

GORDON PARKS
photographer & director

MADAME C.J. WALKER
entrepreneur

MARY MCLEOD BETHUNE
educator

THURGOOD MARSHALL
supreme court justice

KATHERINE DUNHAM
dancer & choreographer

ELIJAH MUHAMMAD
religious leader

ARTHUR ASHE
tennis champion

A. PHILIP RANDOLPH
union leader

W.E.B. DU BOIS
scholar & activist

DIZZY GILLESPIE
musician & bandleader

COUNT BASIE
musician & bandleader

HENRY AARON
baseball player

MEDGAR EVERS
social activist

RAY CHARLES
singer & musician

CRISPUS ATTUCKS
patriot

BILL COSBY
entertainer

ROBERT CHURCH
entrepreneur

CONTENTS

Chapter One

The King
of
the Blues

ITS A SUNDAY afternoon during what will go down in the books as Southern California's hottest September ever—a mind-numbing heat wave. Still, they gather as the hour grows late. The humidity steadily, unmercifully rises. Reporters, protectively huddled under the shade of a brightly covered awning, in full view of the grand open-air stage, swill gratis liquids against the heat.

The anxiety level rises in the milling, anxious, seven thousand-plus, sellout crowd. All eyes occasionally fix on the huge stage for some sign that the headliner, scheduled to close the Michelob beer sponsored two-day

---

B. B. King, in about the mid-sixties, more than a decade after "Three O'Clock Blues" had made him the most popular blues performer in the country. He has often given credit to his white fans for their loyal support over the next three decades.

Fifth Annual Long Beach Blues Festival—
the man they braved the oppressive heat to
hear—is ready to appear.

But there is no sign of the reigning
monarch of the blues, one-time Memphis
Beale Street Blues Boy: *B. B. King!*

Rumors buzz like fat, lazy flies in the
thick, humid air. It is 4:15, and the press
corps is informed that, though due on the
stage at 4 PM, the blues great is still in
transit to the venue. But, no one is certain
whether the "King of the Blues" is sitting in
a limo caught in a gridlock on one of the
many clogged arteries that pose as freeways
in Southern California, or somewhere in the
crowded skies west of Oklahoma.

"He'll never make it," a reporter offers
sadly, more than a twinge of disappointment
in his voice. A woman nearby glares at him.

Others check programs, the crowd, their
time-pieces, then nod in solemn agreement.
They were told a limo, motor running, is
supposed to be waiting for him at the air-
port. With luck it might wind its way
through the Sunday afternoon traffic with
its precious cargo and to the festival site on
the campus of California State University
at Long Beach in record time. But never *on
time.*

All eyes raise the same questions. Will he

be able to perform, if and when, he does arrive? Will he be able to close a festival that has featured the likes of Etta James, John Lee Hooker, Pee Wee Clayton, Jimmy Witherspoon, in the grand fashion that has earned him the right to claim the throne to the Royal Blues Line?

It's Sunday, late, and B.B. King's recent itinerary shows he was in California sometime Wednesday last for a two-day stint in San Diego. Friday, two days later, B.B. headlined a gig nearly a hundred miles north in the broiling San Fernando Valley. And, somehow, he has fulfilled an engagement in *Oklahoma?*

"A workaholic!" someone offers as if the observation explains everything.

"Yeah," another reporter agrees, his voice authoritative as he goes on to explain, "B.B. King does three hundred or more appearances a year!"

"Been doing it for thirty years," comes from another member of the increasingly impatient press corps. The reporter quickly tells the anxious gathering that the pinkie ring B. B. King wears religiously was a gift from his manager after the blues singer completed 342 one-nighters in 1956.

"I don't have to work as hard as I do," B. B. King explained in a 1980 *Jet* magazine interview. "But I couldn't have stopped before, even for a short while, as some of my (friends) pleaded with me to do. If I had stopped back then, the blues would no longer be alive. I hope my kids will forgive me. I hope they will understand why I was never there."

A glance at the faces in the crowd reveals the composition of B. B.'s avid following. They are old and young; representing a diversity of ethnic lines—black, white, Asian, Hispanic, all caught up in the musical magic of the blues as only B. B. King can call them to life.

The nervous conversation turns to B. B.'s illustrious history; beginning with his humble beginnings on a plantation in the lush Mississippi Delta. They recall the mythical tale of the eight dollar guitar presented B. B. at age fourteen by an uncle. They talk of the B. B.'s gospel group, "The Famous St. John Gospel Singers," that sang all over in the churches of the hill country and delta of Mississippi, and in time were broadcast over WGRM radio in Greenwood. And, they mumble the words to B. B.'s 1952 hit, "Three O'clock Blues."

"I used to sing gospel," recalled B. B. in a 1982 interview, "and was pretty good until the girls showed up. The only difference

Etta James, one of the all-time great blues singers. Although she is sometimes said to be difficult, and often spends long periods of time in self-imposed isolation. B. B. admires Etta and has often worked with her; she's a guest artist on two of his C.Ds.

between a gospel and a blues tune was usually the lyrics; they had the same feeling."

It's the "feeling" that this crowd has come to experience, revel in. A feeling that touches all, regardless of race or creed.

In the beginnings of the recordings of the blues, and for several decades afterwards, the blues was a country relative to gospel and was considered loutish, loud, obscene and therefore was condemned as "the devil's music" and was to be shunned by all the more "respectable black folk." Respectable black folk avoided the seamy quarters of Beale Street bistros where B. B. King honed his blues skills in the shadow of the likes of Blind Lemon Jefferson, T-Bone Walker and Lonnie Johnson, not to forget the guidance given by cousin Bukka White, an accomplished blues guitarist in his own right.

B. B. took to the blues early, reshaped it to fit his needs, his style, his unique way of responding to the world around him, and the legend began.

In the prelude to *The Arrival of B. B. King,* author Charles Sawyer observed, "B. B. King certainly is the artist of the first rank, the mainstay of a specific art form, the cultural figure of major importance in our time, the Horatio Alger of the modern South."

In the nearly twenty years since the pub-

John Lee Hooker has been a friend and soul-mate since the early Memphis days. Says B. B. of his friend: "John Lee is sure enough unique and still stands as one of the great poets of the blues." Like King, Hooker is also an admirer of Bonnie Raitt.

In the nearly twenty years since the publication of Charles Sawyer's book (1980) the B. B. King legend has grown to gigantic proportions, nearly equaling that of that ambitious white teenager he used to know on Memphis' Beale Street when they were both just getting started with their musical careers.

The road was hard for B. B. as it was for others who were wooed and won over by the "blues muse." Hamilton Binn wrote, in a 1972 *Ebony* magazine article: "They (blues men) have . . . been the victims of an interracial snobbery—a legacy of the times when the blues was the property of contemptible old men hawking dimes on a street corner. The blues if often seen as an Uncle Tom expression, (were considered) a cowardly admission of impotence and despair . . ."

But, novelist Richard Wright explained in the foreword to Paul Oliver's book, *The Meaning of the Blues,* ". . .the most astonishing part of the blues is that, though replete with a sense of defeat and downheartedness, they are not intrinsically pessimistic; their burden of woe and melancholy is dialectically redeemed through sheer force of sensuality, into an almost exultant affirmation of life, of love, of sex, of movement, of hope." But, Wright added,

Jimmy Witherspoon. He, along with Etta James, John Lee Hooker and Pee Wee Clayton, opened the 1984 Long Beach Blues festival where B. B. King celebrated his 59th birthday. It didn't matter that he was late, not to B. B. King fans!

"All American Negroes do not sing the blues."

B.B King was someone who did sing the blues; and extremely well. From the very beginning, B. B. was on a crusade to preserve rather than defend the blues, saying, "if you're a blues performer, you've got to dress 'em (the blues) up to sell."

Misguided blues "purists" assailed B. B. for "selling out" and distorting the true "blue" sound all those years when only he and a handful of others were performing and recording blues of any sort, often for free or very little money, and some of them had to pay for their recordings and try to sell the results at performances.

Back at the Long Beach Festival, all present agreed that it had been a long row to hoe for B. B. King. Over the years he has taken his music and his message to countless colleges and *countries*. And yet few of them knew just how long and how hard that row had been.

Now, thousands of miles away from Itta Bena, Mississippi, where it all began for B. B. on September 16, 1925, a restless, blues hungry crowd awaits an audience with the "King of the Blues."

Suddenly, like a sweet breeze softening the heat wave, there is the long awaited announcement, "The King is here!" Everything is forgotten. The heat. The wait.

Members of the press corps and photographers rush from the protective shade of the awning into the late afternoon sun. They converge on a roped off area directly before the towering stage as all eyes are lifted to greet the approaching monarch.

B. B. is in great form, showing no sign of jet lag or exhaustion from the endless work schedule and a too far reaching itinerary.

He returns the cheers of the crowd with his patented smile and, suddenly as he has appeared, he is on. His eyes are closed as he begins stroking mournful magic from the strings of his prized guitar, "Lucille."

And the crowd is his.

It's also B. B.'s birthday. His fifty-ninth! It seems that everyone has forgotten, lost as they are in the music. But a cake is presented on stage. And, too soon, the concert is over and B. B. King is again on his way, spreading the "good news," sharing the blues! It seemed at the time, he had reached the peak of his career. Where else could he go from here? Hell, he was just then putting the "pedal to the metal."

That seems like a lifetime ago. As this is being written (an updated revision, actually) in the winter of 1997, B. B. is two years past celebrating his seventieth birthday. As a matter of fact, most of the last two years has been something of a celebration. In 1995, he started off the celebration of his 70 years with the opening of the new B. B.'s Club at Universal Studios' City Walk (with a host of fellow blues musicians and friends), and Memphis-connected celebrities such as Priscilla Presley: He celebrated it again on a visit home to the little Mississippi hill town where he mostly grew up and discovered his musical roots, Kilmichael, and again in his father's home-town, Indianola, where they threw a big birthday bash for him and again at a huge riverside celebration in Memphis in September. And while he has reduced those three hundred plus concert dates per year down to about two-fifty, he is still one of the most active musicians around. Possibly, it can now be said that B. B. has taken his career as far as possible. Don't count on it.

When Charles Sawyer published his book in 1980 B. B. was "the Foremost Blues Singer and Guitarist of Our Time." Now, he is recognized as the foremost blues singer and blues guitarist of ALL time. He's come a long way from the little town of Kilmichael, Mississippi.

On March 17, 1981, B. B. played a concert for the inmates of Sheridan Correctional Center in Chicago, and presented a Gibson left handed guitar to inmate Ron Las Puma. Standing (at left) is Warden Neal MacDonald, and Dave Harding of Gibson Guitar.

Chapter Two

A King
Is Born

THE "KING OF THE BLUES" was born under less than regal circumstances, and there has always been a question of exactly where he made his entrance into this world. "Officially" his birth took place on a cotton plantation in the lush Mississippi Delta near Itta Bena and about twenty miles east of Indianola, his father Albert's home town. Later, the story would be told that his mother, Nora Ella, was on a visit to her mother's home near Kilmichael, a farming community eighty miles directly east in the Mississippi hill country, when he was born. As a matter of fact, in his 1980 book, *The Arrival of*

Indianola, Mississippi. While he never actually lived in Indianola until he was in his late teens, the town has always claimed him as their own (ever since he got famous as B. B. King, that is.) Actually, a couple of other towns have a better claim on him.

B. B. King, Charles Sawyer published a photograph he'd shot himself two years earlier which was identified as "Birthplace of Riley B. King, on the bank of Bear Creek, Kilmichael, Mississippi." A relative of B. B.'s recently (1995) told one of our researchers, "That was where he was born, true enough. Nora Ella was up here because she and Albert were having some problems in their marriage. They got word to Albert and he came right up here and got them. That old house's not out there anymore." Wherever the birth took place, it was a natural birth, though it was recalled later that the midwife was late for the blessed moment.

The birth date, September 16, 1925, was recorded a few days later in the Delta town of Indianola, which has always claimed him as a "native son" although the people in Kilmichael "know better" and he did spend most of his growing years in the little hill town. Whatever, it was an inauspicious day and the days of his life would continue to be so until the manchild born that day, Riley B. King, realized his royal bloodline was black and deep *blue*!

But that would be later, much later, after he had paid enough dues, after he had truly become *the* expert in the blues, defined by African American writer Ralph Ellison as

A delta tenet house near Indianola. Actually this one is probably larger than the one in which Riley B. King was born about twenty miles east, over near Itta Bena. But his father registered his birth in Indianola, and Itta Bena, somehow, lost the claim to him.

"an impulse to keep the painful details and episodes of a brutal experience alive in one's aching consciousness to finger its jagged grain, and to transcend it . . . by squeezing from it a near-tragic, near-comic lyricism." Young Riley B. King had much to learn, to suffer, to transcend.

His father, Albert King, was reared by a black sharecropper named Major Love and his wife Kathleen with whom he had been left by his older brother, also named Riley, following the death of both their mother and her sister, their only known kin. Their father had disappeared soon after Albert's birth. From all accounts, the Love family was kind to Albert. When he was about the age of seven, Albert was told that his brother was an inmate in a Texas prison. He never heard from him or anything more about him after that.

Albert had no education.. The Loves, like most Delta sharecroppers, could not afford the luxury of educating their ward. However, he was skilled—a competent tractor driver and mechanic, vital skills in an agrarian economy. For a work shift lasting from sun-to-sun (sun up to sun down) he would earn fifty cents. Often, in the hurry of the planting season, he worked two shifts.

When the young girl who would become

Chopping cotton, 1937. One of the poignant photographs taken by Dorothea Lang for the Farm Security Administration, about the time Riley B. King was doing his share of chopping cotton. Lang's photographs are available in book form as are others.

the mother of B. B. King, Nora Ella Farr, moved to the Delta from Kilmichael with her family, she was in her mid-teens and Albert was only a year older (he was only eighteen when Riley was born). Nora Ella was a staunchly religious young woman, daughter of a strict, puritanical family, the base of which was the sanctified holiness church.

After a brief courtship the young couple were married and set up housekeeping in a sharecropper's cabin on a plantation near Itta Bena. The Farr family missed their relatives and friends and the familiar and "more friendly" hill country they'd left behind.. Not long after Nora Ella was married, they moved back to Kilmichael to live. Nora Ella was quite close to her family, and while she knew she would miss them, she also knew they would always offer support in times of trouble. And troubled times were not long in coming.

The couple raised most of their food by truck farming on a small plot of land on the Itta Bena plantation owned by a man named Jim O'Reilly while Albert drove a tractor for cash wages. As with most young couples in that time and place it was difficult to make ends meet from week to week.

It was the mid nineteen-twenties and most

of America was still in recovery from World War I. African Americans were on the move. It was a period of upheaval, of frustration and even *hope:* a period which would be referred to by historians as the "Great Migration."

Many African Americans shook the dust of the South from their boot heels and headed north in hopes of a better and brighter future. They traveled in caravans. Hopped freight trains. Out of Mississippi, it was the Illinois Central, Chicago bound through Memphis. Out of New Orleans, Louisiana and Texas it was, for the most part, the Union Pacific, bound for Los Angeles.

They just *left,* taking with them little more than hopes and dreams that somewhere in America they would find freedom from the poverty and sometimes violent oppression that plagued them in the South. Where reconstruction seemed to offer some hope in the beginning, eventually it brought only more trouble. Many of the Northerners that flocked to the South following the South's defeat were less than honest, both those who came in a government capacity, and those that just came to loot and steal.

Families who had not seen any real money in years suddenly found themselves faced with unpayable tax bills and unable to borrow money on land that was long ago bought

By the 1990s, Indianola's claim to B. B. King has come to be taken as "the truth and nothing but" no matter what those residents of Kilmichael, eighty miles to the east, up in the hills where he grew up, or Itta Bena (again) twenty miles to the east,

where he was born nearby, or even Memphis, have to say about it. For one thing there is a street named after B. B. in Indianola that runs right past Gentry high school. Too, this the true blues land where the former Riley B. King chooses to play concerts.

and paid for. The banks and the law were in the pockets of Northern "carpetbaggers." A large segment of the population, both black and white, was reduced to eating roots and berries, and forging in the woods. It should be remembered that Grant's Union army crisscrossed Mississippi three times, beginning in 1862 not long after the war began and each time leaving both large plantations and small family farms devastated without food or farm animals to produce more. The central hill country that surrounded the Kilmichael area was home to mostly small family farms, and very few of those owned slaves and then often only one and seldom more than a family of five to ten. But those out in the countryside were a bit better off than the city dwellers. Jackson, for instance, was burned to the ground by the Union Army three times until it came to be called Chimmyville, a name it carried for decades.

The Reconstruction laws were applied just as harshly there as elsewhere. One might ask why whites would, as they did, vote their former slaves into office. "That choice," wrote one prominent Mississippi historian, "was preferable to those whites sent from the north to rule." Still, families were put out of houses in which they'd lived for generations and often former slaves who had been hired to remain and work for wages, found that the new owners were worse "slave drivers" than any of the old overseers had been. The situation was explosive and explode it did throughout the South. This horror brought about such organizations as the Ku Klux Klan and also the Jim Crow laws. Although blacks were elected to public office in the beginning, even in some areas where whites were allowed the vote, the situation was made intolerable for both races. The Reconstructionists didn't want peace; they wanted to get rich on the backs of both black and white Southerners. Many of them did and you can still visit small Southern towns today and be pointed out representatives of families who have been there some 130 years and be told "of course they come from carpetbaggers." They never have and never will be totally accepted by Southerners, black or white, no matter how rich and "social" some of them have become or how many Country Club and other social organizations they buy their way into.

But at the time, the situation only served to create more troubles between blacks and whites (Q: "where is my mule and forty acres?" (A: "That crooked tax bandit just took my last forty acres, including my house and my wife's truck garden. Took her mule, too.")

In areas where settlements were few and far between--especially after the War, troubles reached out in all directions. And trouble was what those in charge wanted. First it came in the form of Ku Klux Klan raids on both whites and blacks who were not "behaving themselves." And next it came under the name of Jim Crow, named after an old "black face" musical carnival character.

Still, at the time of Riley's birth, Albert and his teenage bride were struggling with the rich Delta soil for enough of its bounty to live in an area still cursed by the back-breaking poverty that was magnified a hundred times by a Civil War and Grant's "scorched earth" policy. It was said that after his army marched from Jackson east to Atlanta, they left a stretch of land fifty miles wide "that would not support a single crow."

The economic recovery following the recent World War I did not make it much past the Mason-Dixon line. African Americans, offered false promises and given the hope of a better life, were, by the time of Riley King's birth, leaving the South by the hundreds and thousands.

Historians offer many reasons for the "Great Migration" of the twenties. There was the lure of jobs in the steel mills of the North. There was the failing economy in the South. There was the hope of escaping from the violent hand of the Ku Klux Klan, which had reared up with a new vengeance at the end of World War I. And, as important, there was the thirst for freedom and prosperity African Americans hoped to find in the supposedly "free" cities of the North.

Sadly, African Americans did not find that freedom and prosperity they had hoped for. Instead they found the same racial discrimination they had faced in the South. Refugees, they were forced to find housing in the already substandard and overcrowded segregated communities in the North. And there were no jobs. Many freedom-seeking African Americans spent their first winters in the North jobless in cramped substandard quarters.

Still, these migrating African Americans took with them, along with too quickly shattered hopes and dreams, their religious views, their songs, their culture. And these elements contributed greatly to the artistic achievements of the Harlem Renaissance of the 1920s as African American artists—writers, actors, painters and musicians—

searched for an African American identity.

The mid-twenties was an exciting era for African American art and music in parts of the nation. And it was also a period of extraordinary activity on the part of black artists which coincided with a time of extraordinary receptivity on the part of the white public, reaching a peak in the mid twenties. And, while poor and often illiterate share-croppers toiled in the oppressive sun of the deep South, northern blacks and whites were celebrating a so-called art and literary awakening among the sons and daughters of slaves, now expressing themselves through bold artistic statements. Writers such as Claude McKay, (*Harlem Shadows*, 1922), Alain Locke, (*The New Negro,* 1925), Langston Hughes, *The Weary Blues* 1926) and others were at an artistic peak as were numerous jazz and blues musicians.

However, all this activity would remain unknown to the first born of the King family for at least a decade, and not fully realized until he was a grown man. He was named Riley B, in memory of Albert's long missing brother and also for Jim O'Reilly, who had been fair and kind to Albert and his little family. The B didn't stand for anything unless it was "Blessed" for in a way the baby was but it would be many years before he realized God had bestowed a most unique gift to him.

When Nora Ella's second-born, also a son, died in infancy, the marriage fell apart. Riley was four when Nora Ella, still a young girl, got word to one of her uncles to come and get her and little Riley and take them home to Kilmichael. They left Albert standing in the yard of the little cabin outside Itta Bena. It would be the last time Riley would see his father for quite some time, and years before he would live with him again in his father's house and then for only a short time that would turn out terrible and leave him both disappointed and humiliated.

For the next few years he would know only his mother's family, a large but close-knit group who looked after one another in both good times and bad. For the most part the family worked on the farms of three white men, Edwayne Henderson, George Booth, and Flake Cartledge, although one of Riley's aunts did day work for Ira and Letty Palmertree, and that would, eventually, lead Riley to the acquiring of his first guitar from Mrs. Palmertree's nephew, Denzil Tidwell.

Kilmichael was a close-knit community where everyone knew just about everyone else. Nearby, only about five miles down a

Itta Bena is a charming little town, somewhat prettier and about half the size of Indianola. The name is a Choctaw word that has something to do with woods and water, perhaps a cypress swamp? There are plenty of those around. And Itta Bena has a

"king" of its own to celebrate. Jerry Rice played his college football at Mississippi Valley State University! Right there in Itta Bena. Oddly, Moorhead, halfway between the Indianola and Itta Bena was the setting for W. C. Handy's *Yellow Dog Blues*.

country road, near the community of Poplar Creek, Oprah Winfrey's father was growing up on the farm his family had owned for generations. The Winfreys were "well off" and deeply respected by both black and whites but Riley's people were just poor "common folks," who had to toil for others to earn their living. Being separated from his mother was to be Riley's next lesson in the blues.

A Mississippi delta cypress swamp. The entire delta was once covered with such swamps, reaching, as William Faulkner once said (but another writer said it before him) "from the lobby of the Peabody hotel in Memphis to Catfish Row in Vicksburg," and covering about a quarter of the state. Because of the swamps, there was very little agriculture in the delta until the Chinese were imported in the 1850s to drain them. Their work was interrupted by the Civil War and it was not until a decade later that the "richest soil in the world" was growing cotton. The Chinese? It seemed they came to own every grocery store in the delta at one time; and many of them are still there. And with Southern accents as deep as most other customers at the Golden Dragon in Greenwood, said by one national magazine to be the "best Chinese restaurant in the country!"

Chapter Three

Grandma's Hands

IN OCTOBER OF 1929, the year Nora Ella went back to the hills to live, the nation's stock market crashed. There was panic in the upper circles of American finance. What would come to be known as the Great Depression brought severe hardship and deprivation to America.

The Great Depression did not make a great difference, one way or another, to most of the people around Kilmichael. It was, in those days (and to a great extent, still is) a farming community, a place where the country people raised their own food. In those days, they came into town on Saturday to do the weekly shopping and, for the young

The Reverend Archie Fair and his wife. To young Riley, Fair, a sanctified preacher at the Pinkney Grove Church of God in Christ was "like a God." It was Fair that encouraged Riley's interest in singing and, especially the guitar and working with him singing.

an afternoon and evening that seemed almost like a holidays. Young country kids, both white and black, played on the large sandy lot that lay between the Columbus & Greenville train depot on the south side, and the block-long tree-shaded hitching rail which accommodated farm wagons on the north. The town was (and is) but two rows of stores, one to the north, facing south across the sandy lot to where the old C&G station used to be; the second row of stores faced the east, creating a L-shape. A second street behind that on the west was home to the black cafes and other black-owned businesses. Any courting the young people had to do was mostly done on those Saturday forays to town with the family, or the next day at church.

Young Riley's grandmother, Elnora Farr, sharecropped on the farm owned by a tall, distinguished looking man named Edwayne Henderson, who also kept about 40 or 50 dairy cows. His farm, which B. B. would remember as a "plantation" was located about two miles east of Kilmichael on highway 82. The area around Kilmichael was and is "cow country," now known for its pure breed cattle ranches. "Back then," says one old timer, "it was mostly dairy cattle and there was three different places you could

The Edwayne Henderson farm, a couple miles east of Kilmichael, where young Riley's grandmother, Elnora Farr, sharecropped. B. B. King can't remember ever living there but he did go visit often and to work at times, or so Henderson's records indicate.

sell your milk, including the Carnation plant in Winona (the county seat, ten miles to the west). If I remember correctly old man Henderson was one of the first around here to put in electric milkers." Also employed and living at Henderson's place at the time was Riley's aunt, Mima Stells, and his uncles, Jesse Davidson and William Pulley.

It has been said that Henderson worked every bit as hard as the people who were employed by him. On at least one occasion, during the lean years of the depression, he borrowed money from the bank, putting up his farm as collateral, to feed his own family and those eight or so families who worked for him.

Grandmother Elnora's life revolved around the strict teachings of fundamentalist religion, which she sternly passed on to her grandson Riley, once she got the chance. Meanwhile, for a few years, young Riley still had his mother, who went on to have two more husbands in her short life. He did not hear from his father very often after his parents separated, except for a couple of trips he and his mother took to Indianola to visit the Loves on the bus. In those days eighty miles was a long trip and especially for a man such as Albert who could not afford the luxury of an automobile.

Nora Ella did not move in with her mother and other relatives on the Henderson place upon her return to Kilmichael. She moved into a small cabin on the farm of a man named Flake Cartledge, about six miles southeast of Kilmichael, the other side of the Big Black River swamp near the French Camp road, where she did day work, sometimes helping out in the house. "Mr. Flake" as B. B. still refers to him, was said to be blind to racial distinctions.

B. B. later said he never heard Cartledge ever use the word "nigger" and seemed uncomfortable around those who did. He never referred to Riley as "boy" but either called him by his first name or "Son." While Riley had his chores assigned to him, he was also encouraged to enroll at the Baptist Church operated Elkhorn School, about two miles away, run by an extraordinary man named Luther Henson.

At any rate, Elnora Farr was back and forth between the Henderson place and the Cartledge farm for the next few years, making her presence felt in Riley's life.

Relatives recall that it was not long after Nora Ella came back from the Delta that she "took up" with her second husband, a man named Ed Basket.

However, it was in his grandmother's

Kilmichael (one of three small towns with that name; the others are in Scotland and Ireland) is a small farming community that time has passed by. At one time the streets were crowded on Saturday when farmers from the area came into town to shop and

visit. The town began to lose its business to Winona, a much larger town ten miles to the east, in the 1950s, where retailers were more progressive. The movie theater was the building to the left of the bank. There was a balcony for "the colored."

world of religious fundamentalism and hard
work that young Riley grew to learn the fun-
damentals and true meaning of the blues.
There was an uneasy kinship between religious music and the blues. Often the only
telling difference was the lyrics themselves.

There were work songs that bellowed from
the strong throats of those men and women
who labored in the fields.

There was the music that "rocked" the
members of Holiness Church, which his
grandmother attended, into spiritual frenzy.

And there was "devil music," the blues!

Riley King was introduced to the music
which would be the foundation of his blues
through the religion subscribed to by both
his mother and grandmother.

His powerful and expressive singing voice
was first discovered by Reverend Archie
Fair, a Sanctified Preacher, who was pastor
at the Pinkney Grove Church of God in
Christ which most of Elnora Farr's family
faithfully attended.

Riley's musical bent was quickly discovered by Reverend Fair, and it wasn't long
before he became a featured singer at
church services (as well as a Sunday School
teacher to the younger children). Reverend
Fair's faith in Riley's talent prompted him
to give the lad his first guitar lessons.

The music at Pinkney Grove was animated, expressive, soul searching and cathartic. It offered hope and life. It offered a release for bottled up emotions.

"There is no music like that music," wrote James Baldwin, African American essayist/novelist, "no drama like the drama of the saints rejoicing, the sinner moaning, the tambourines racing, and all those voices coming together and crying holy unto the Lord. I have never seen anything to equal the fire and excitement that sometimes, without warning, fill a church, causing the church . . . to *rock!*"

"Rock" didn't exactly mean the same thing in Riley's day's at Pinkney Grove as the word does now, or perhaps it did, but without the secular aspects it has taken on in modern times.

However, that church music was essential to Riley's development as a blues artist. It was out of the music of the church, Gospel and its variations, that the blues was spawned. W.C. Handy, (who died in 1915), considered the "Father of the Blues," acknowledged the importance of the folk songs and religious songs in the creation of his blues, saying, "Each of my Blues is based on some old Negro song of the South, some old song that is part of the memories of my

The old Pinkney Grove Church of God in Christ, a holiness church which Riley King's grandmother and her entire family looked on as the very center of their lives. Riley's uncle, William Pullian, was married to the sister of the Pentecostal

Sanctified Minister of the church, Archie Fair. Fair became a strong influence in young Riley's life. Not long after Riley left the Kilmichael area and went out to become B. B. King, the old church building above was replaced by a new building.

childhood and my race."

In the church, African American worshippers might sing out "My Lord calls me,/He calls me by the thunder,/the trumpet sounds it in my soul." And the power of the singing fairly convulsed all present.

And, work songs helped pass the long hours in the field and on "chain gangs" as they sang out:

  Take this hammer—huh!
  And carry it to the captain—huh!
  You tell him I'm gone—huh!
  If he asks you—huh!
  Was I runnin'—huh!
  You tell him I was flyin'—huh!
  Tell him I was flyin'—huh!

The songs were rhythmic, often bitter. sometimes humorous. They expressed what the singers felt, what they saw. They were a direct link to Africa where there were songs for all occasions—birth, work, play, war and death. The tradition was held over and the songs became important as a method of coping with the indignities of slavery.

And, from the steamy innards of "juke joints," ramshackle nightclubs, where workers escaped their troubles, sprang the blues.

The blues was a plaintive cry against a troubled life.

I laid down last night,
Turning from side to side;
Yes, I was turning from side to side,
I was not sick,
I was just dissatisfied.
When I got up this mornin',
Blues walking round my bed;
Yes, the blues was walkin' round my bed
I went to eat my breakfast.
The blues was all in my bread.

For Riley, the music, both religious and secular, provided a world view and means of self-expression, a platform from which to speak his deepest feelings. And, his involvement with the blues seemed a natural progression. Though times were difficult for African Americans in the deep South, the birthplace of the blues, the blues was making major strides as a commercial product.

The southern blues took on a new form and dimension. It was an organic music, adaptable to all situations. It was soon "urbanized" to cope with the new experience in the north.

It's a sign on the building, yes, I mean, you hear me sing,

There's a sign on the building, we all got
to move right away,
I ain't got no money, no rent that I can
pay.
It soon will be cold, you hear me sing, yes,
I mean,
It soon will be cold, I ain't got no place to
go,
I'm going back south, where the chilly
winds don't blow.

But those who returned to the south found
that things were no better.

It was in 1920 that the funky blues began
to gain a wider and more mainstream audience. Mamie Smith recorded Perry
Bradford's "Crazy Blues" on the Okeh
Records Label and the era of "race records"
began. The recording quickly caught on and
sold an amazing 7,500 copies per week for
months.

Black recording artists were "discovered",
recorded and marketed, almost overnight, to
satisfy the avid interest in the funky blues
music. Ma Rainey, Jelly Roll Morton, Bessie
Smith, Billie Holiday, Ella Fitzgerald,
Muddy Waters, and many, many others
quickly became household names among
both blacks and whites.

Stars were born! Heroes and heroines of

The great Paul Robeson once declared "One great creation, modern popular music, whether it be in theatre, film, radio, records—whatever it may be—is almost completely based upon Negro idiom." He insisted all popular singers were influenced.

song who expressed the uniqueness of the black experience in terms African Americans took to heart. Whites, too, found a power in and an attraction to the blues oozing like hot lava from the tinny horn-speakers of Gramophones..

Black music, wrote scholar W.E.B. Du Bois, "has not only influenced American music, it has influenced American life. It has become the popular medium for our national expression musically. And who can say that it does not express the blare and jangle and the surge, too, of our national spirit?"

The great Paul Robeson, who gained national attention for his scholastics, his athletic ability, his singing and his acting, once declared "One great creation, modern popular music, whether it be in theatre, film, radio, records—whatever it may be— is almost completely based upon the Negro idiom. There is no leading American singer, performer of popular songs, whether it be Crosby, a Sinatra, a Shore, a Judy Garland, an Ella Logan, who has not listened—and learned—by the hour to Holiday, Waters, Florence Mills, to Bert Williams, to Fitzgerald, and to the greatest of all, Bessie Smith." Fifties pop icon Johnnie Ray never forgot to acknowledge his debt to Billie

Holiday. As a child he'd listened to his sister's collection of Holiday records for hours on end.

There was music in Riley's family. Both parents sang, his mother the rousing church songs that rocked the faithful; his father those dirty, "devil songs," the blues, which somehow freed the spirit.

Riley's Aunt Mima had a record player, and a collection of records that included the recordings of Blind Lemon Jefferson and Lonnie Johnson, who, rather than the Mississippi Delta blues singers, were the early blues influences on Riley. Too, his Uncle Jack Bennett, who lived nearby, was a blues shouter. Aunt Mima had a rather large collection of records and it included all the popular singers of the day: Ma Rainey, Mamie Smith, Bessie Smith, Duke Ellington and even some of the popular country artists of the time. But it was still the blues that commanded Riley's attention the most.

And the blues, once the music became popular enough for the press to take note, became a cause of conflict and contention among those, both black and white, who saw the blues as "devil music" which would somehow corrupt them all. They did not care that the blues was based on the same expressive rhythms as more religious songs.

Writer Robert Palmer observed in the Los Angeles *Herald Examiner* newspaper that "Many whites believed the segregationist literature that warned of 'primitive jungle rhythms' corrupting the morals of the South's white youths."

There were those African Americans who also hated the dirty blues. "To churchgoing and community-minded blacks," wrote Palmer, "blues was the devil's music, and an embarrassment because the uneducated black sharecroppers and day laborers who drank illicit moonshine whiskey, gambled, and played, listened or danced to the blues were at the very bottom of the Delta's social pyramid. They were the sort of people who seemed determined to give respectable Mississippi blacks a bad name."

Riley loved both the religious and secular music that surrounded him. It was more than entertainment. The music told stories that were in no books available to Riley. The music offered direction, expressed purpose and hope. It was the throbbing heart and living soul of a people. A people's history, past, present and future, put to music.

Much later, as the reigning King of the Blues, B. B. would explain that the "blues isn't just some sad music about a broken heart, a busted dream, or a painful love affair. Blues is much more than any of these things. If I could pick three descriptions of it, I'd say it ain't nothing but living, laughing and loving."

It was a cathartic music. A music that laughed and cried, too, allowing a full range of human emotions to be experienced through the story line. Yes, the blues also told stories, some real, some fantastic fantasies, but all, in a sense, true.

"When the blues started," B. B. explains, "a lot of times, the songs didn't really mean that the old lady left the man or the house had burned down. It meant something far beyond that."

There was a hidden message in the music, known only, sometimes, to the blues singer or a small cadre of blues aficionados who "understood."

This tendency to be dark and mysterious was also a hold over from earlier folk songs and work songs which, though berating masters and whites in general, were often couched in language and imagines understood only by African Americans. It was a secret language founded in their personal and peculiar experiences in America.

During slavery, the song "Steal Away" was said to have been used as a warning to slaves that Harriet Tubman's Underground

Railroad would be moving north that night.

The following passage reflects the duplicity that often adds deeper meaning to the blues:

Well, I drink to keep from worrying and I laugh to keep from crying (sung twice)
I keep a smile on my face so that the pub lic won't know my mind.
Some people thinks I am happy but they sho' don't know my mind (twice)
They see this smile on my face, but my heart is bleeding all the time.

And, though there were only those certain African Americans who could read between the lines (all African Americans don't sing or like the blues), the blues had a spirit, power and story line to which people across color lines could relate. It was often simple, earthy wisdom.

But it was still too early in Riley's development for him to really play the blues. He was learning, through experience, note for note, moanful groan for moanful groan, each adding another mournful note to what would become B. B. King's musical vocabulary.

"I remember my childhood," he told a reporter, "how things were with us then, the race problems and how bad it was in the 1930s. There was tragedies I experienced I could never talk about, so it all just stayed with me. And so the did the blues."

There was another blues influence early on in Riley's life. Bukka White, the "king of the slide guitar" was Nora Ella's first cousin and had also grown up in Kilmichael. He lived in Memphis and always returned home to visit at Christmas (with presents!) and often in mid-summer when the crops were laid by and the workers had free time to visit. By the time Riley was living there, Bukka (Booker T. Washington) White was cutting records for RCA Victor, having moved up from his original label, Vocalion.

He took young Riley under his wing and encouraged his interest in the guitar. But at the time Riley was, like everyone else, more impressed by the expensive automobile, fancy clothing and tales of playing in night-clubs as far away as Chicago.

Still the lesson that some people made a living playing music, and obviously a very good one, was not lost on the young man from Kilmichael.

Chapter Four

One-Room Schoolhouse

EDUCATION IN AN agricultural community was for the rich, most especially the Mississippi of the 1920s and 1930s. The limited education available to the children of African American sharecroppers and tenant farmers was seasonal, dependent on planting and harvesting seasons. Often there would be two school sessions within a year, one during the winter, and a second, shorter term in mid-summer after the crops had been laid by. However, Kilmichael had long boasted two high schools (Big Black, named after the nearby river, was for white students and Mt. Zion was for "the colored" and scattered about the countryside were public

Luther Henson, headmaster at the one-room Elkhorn Baptist School where Riley obtained all of his formal education. Henson was a remarkable man, admired by most blacks and whites who lived in the area. His influence on Riley was immeasurable.

secondary schools for both white and black, separate but anything but equal.

Young Riley King was fortunate in that about two miles from the Flake Cartledge place was located the private Elkhorn School, just across from and kept by the Elkhorn Baptist Church.

Beginning soon after he and Nora Ella moved from the Delta and took up residence on the Cartledge place, Riley started attending Elkhorn. After he'd finished his morning chores (which including milking ten cows as soon as he was old enough to handle that job) he'd walk the nearly two miles to Elkhorn School, rain or shine. Of course if there was a ride offered, he'd take that too.

He was never a superior student but from the beginning he was serious about school.

"Luther Henson was the one man who could knock some sense in my head," he recalled years later.

Luther Henson had a reputation for being able to knock, or at least coerce, sense into a lot of heads. A remarkable man of boundless energy, his was a one-room country school that attracted some forty to fifty students each year, from pre-primer to 12th grade.

Henson commanded the respect of many

Luther Henson's Elkhorn "school in the woods." It is now used for other purposes (community house for the church, etc.), and is no longer operated as a school. Students now attend Montgomery County schools at Kilmichael, some seven miles across the river.

local whites, such as Flake Cartledge, and the "little school out in the woods" received a modicum of support from that community as well as from the church membership.

Luther was more concerned about education than money or property. Unable to attend any of the local historically black colleges, Luther was able to raise enough money to attend Rust College, a Methodist supported black institution in Holly Springs, Mississippi, but only for a year.

Luther Henson's formal education was finished with with the completion of correspondence courses from Rust, then he turned to the black press and the writings of a strong black literati, novelists and poets, to keep his mind fresh and his students' interests high. He hoped to convince them that they could, no matter how impossible it might seem, rise above their status even in the face of Jim Crow racial oppression and violence.

The young teacher told his charges of the gains that were being made by African Americans in the mid 1930s. There were young men such as Thurgood Marshall fighting racism in the nation's court; and others such as Jesse Owens, making history and battling racism in the world of sports.

punches when it came to teaching his students about the unfairness of the system, particularly the unequal school system that then existed in Mississippi. And he told them of the violent history of the state and that of the local area. But he also reminded them that "not all white people are bad...bad people come in all colors."

His lessons were not in vain; one of his students would become Montgomery County's first black sheriff and another would become the superintendent of Montgomery County High School at Kilmichael after it was integrated in the 1960s. Henson risked his life for what he believed, for what he hoped his young charges would not only come to believe but accomplish. He knew, as Dr. Martin Luther King Jr. would teach later, "dreams can and will come true. . .with a little effort!"

Life for Riley and his kin was often bleak. Fortunately they worked for two men, Henderson and Cartledge, who had a reputation for being honest and fair with those who worked for them. Sharecropping was a tedious business and while some families could end up with as much as twenty-five hundred dollars in profit at the end of the year, other, smaller families, could end up with nothing, or worse, owing the landown-

Rust College in Holly Springs, Mississippi. A member of the Henson family says that Luther Henson sold land left him by his father in order to attend Rust for one session. Thereafter he relied on correspondence courses from Rust as well as books, pamplets,

magazines and newspapers for his education and to pass on information to his students. Henson was a major influence in Riley King's life, as he was with practically all his students. He was very popular in the black community and among many whites.

er.

Riley and Nora Ella were given a small cabin in which to live that was located quite near the Cartledge family home, a typical small farmhouse that, then, had only two bedrooms and no indoor plumbing. Flake and Thelma Cartledge were young, having been married only a year or so before. Later, when their only child, Wayne, was born, Nora Ella helped Thelma around the house for which she was paid $15 a week. Nora Ella had other chores; there were times when every hand, including that of Thelma, was needed in the fields. Riley had his own chores to perform before and after school.

Luther Henson's niece remembers that Elkhorn school was in session from late September until about the middle of March. A short summer session was held in mid summer which concentrated on Bible studies for the most part. It was after all, a religious-supported institution.

The relationship between Nora Ella and Ed Basket was short-lived. When Riley was about eight, she took up with a man who lived in the lovely little village of French Camp about eight miles down the road to the southeast on the historic Natchez Trace.

However, Nora Ella had little time to enjoy either the bucolic setting or her new relationship. Her health had already begun to fail when she left Riley with his grandmother, and after her move, the progression of her ailment was drastic and serious.

It is not clear if Riley went to live with his grandmother, Elnora Farr, on the Henderson place or if she came out to Nations to live with him, when Nora Ella took her leave for French Camp. B. B. King remembers living with Elnora for only a short time but he does not recall that he was with her at her house at that time. As a matter of fact, he does not recall ever living at Edwayne Henderson's place, just going there for brief periods of time to visit and stay with relatives, sometimes to work for short periods when they were unusually busy. Henderson's accounts ledger places him there in 1940 but that could have been for only a very short time.

It is more likely they were at the Cartledge place when word came that Nora Ella was extremely ill and not expected to live. That she had gone blind over a short time in the months before her death suggests she had untreated diabetes. A doctor had been called but he could only treat Nora Ella's pain and give comfort to the family.

After a few days Elnora took her little grandson back home and waited for the word that came in the night, about two weeks later, that his kind, warm, fun-loving mother, really the only family he had known, was dying. They traveled back to French Camp and arrived in time for Riley to hold her hand and talk to his mother. She told him that if he would always be kind to people and respect them, he would do fine in life.

For Riley, the funeral and burial at Pinkney Grove, was almost unbearable. Several relatives, and especially Elnora, offered Riley a home. But he didn't want to live with his relatives. Then Flake Cartledge came up with a plan. He offered to let Riley live in the little cabin he'd shared with his mother and invited him to take his meals with the Cartledge family.. He also took on his mother's duties in the house, along with working in the fields, and helped Flake Cartledge with his road grading, which he did for the county for extra cash.

B. B. has often expressed his eternal gratitude to the man he still refers to as "Mr. Flake," who saw the hurt he carried after the death of his mother and left him alone in the little cabin to work out his pain. He was within earshot of "Mr. Flake's house" and had nothing to fear but the memories

Pinkney Grove cemetery where B. B. King's mother is buried. Her death all but paralyzed him with grief, calmed some by the offer of "Mr. Flake" to let him continue to live in the cabin they'd shared. He would take his meals with Mr. Flake's family.

that came in the night. Riley remembered later that some of his relatives, living nearby, were not so kind to him.

It was not long after Riley moved into the cabin that he arranged to buy his first "real" guitar from Denzil Tidwell for $15. The most recent account of this transaction has him arranging with "Mr. Flake" to advance him the money and withhold it from his salary in two payments of $7.50.* About a year later the guitar was stolen from the cabin. Riley found it impossible to understand how anyone could take something that meant so much to him. It was about this time that he, too, began hitching a ride into Kilmichael every Wednesday night. That was the night, during the warm months, they set up a movie projector and screen in Mr. Austin's pasture and showed "movies for the colored," although quite a few whites were always also in attendance because the nearest real theatre was ten miles away in Winona (it had a balcony, as did most movie houses in the South, for "the colored.")

Most of the movies were Westerns and among Riley's favorites were the films of Gene Autry, the singing cowboy "who always got the girl," Tex Ritter and Wild Bill Elliott, and sometimes the productions produced at the time "for the colored" by Oscar

Micheaux and others. The Wednesday night movies, playing his guitar, and school made it possible for him to cope.

Riley tried to learn to play by listening to the records of Blind Lemon Jefferson and Lonnie Johnson on his Aunt Mima's record player but he wasn't ready for the blues.

But it was Archie Fair, the Sanctified Preacher Archie Fair who taught him the E, A, and B chords basic to all gospel music. He still had the gospel music at church and, besides, church was where the girls were.

He formed a vocal quartet with his cousin Birkett Davis and two classmates, Dubois Hume and Walter Doris, Jr. They called themselves the Elkhorn Jubilee Singers and soon had an avid following, playing and singing at most of the local churches at one time or another.

And, though Riley may not have considered it at the time, he was in training for "singing and playing the blues."

In spite of his home with kindly Flake Cartledge, who always called him by his name or "son" and Luther Henson's school and Archie Fair's church, Riley was still lonely. Lonely but happy. He was thirteen and the world didn't seem so bad after all.

As B. B. King has said, "Mr. Flake (Cartledge) didn't have a racist bone in his

At the time Riley was living with the Flake Cartledge family he often walked the seven or so miles into Kilmichael, to visit his Grandmother Elnora, and also to attend the movies on Wednesday nights in Mr. Austin's pasture. At that time the road

was unpaved and differed little from Winfrey road, above. It is a few miles to the south. Oprah Winfrey's grandparents lived on this road. Their house (and most of the others on the road) is gone now but the Winfrey cemetery and ruined church is there.

body." There were such white men, and families, around. And the southern half of Montgomery County was home to more than it's share of them. Oprah Winfrey's family farm was surrounded by white farmers and timber men.

The large and clannish Palmertree family and their friends and relatives by marriage, Canons, Montagues, Gibsons, Parkersons, Austins, and others owned most of the land surrounding the Winfrey farm and many of them had, over the years, became friends and protectors of the Winfreys and the nearby Bennett, Henson, and the few other African American families down there.

Said one informant, "Those Palmertrees had a reputation for being wild and a bit untamed--my grandfather used to joke that they were on hand to cook a Thanksgiving dinner when the first Choctaw Indians showed up here. There were about four branches of them, descended from two brothers and their sons who moved here while the Indians were still here. The only way you could make a living here then was with the permission of the Choctaws, as traders or whatever and it's said a couple of those men married Choctaw women and picked up the Choctaw custom of treating others fairly. Even today you can tell the ones that came from the Choctaws by the eyes. It's in the eyes. And they were independent as they could be. One of them was a judge or something and went to Federal prison rather then prosecute his neighbors for making whiskey on their own land.

"They were a wild bunch, some of them, but they were fair and I know they'd hire a colored man to work for them as soon as they would a white man and treat them fair and square. The colored respected that and for that some white people looked down on them. Some of them were great believers in education and not only sent their own off to college but loaned money to their friends to send their kids to college. One old man who'd sent several to college, died a few years ago and left $17 million, huge tracts of timberland and owned the majority of stock in a local bank. There were these sort of people and there were others, just the opposite, people who was just as racist as you could get.

"Some of the Palmertrees attended singings at the church presided over by the Winfrey preachers for generations but were members of nearby Friendship Methodist and Hebron Baptist church, or any of a dozen white churches in the surrounding countryside." Says Mrs. Margette Grice (nee

Palmertree), "We'd often attend the services because Reverend Winfrey was an excellent preacher. I remember a lot of my relatives attending and the Hunts, and my husband's family, the Grices."

Riley was sixteen and the world didn't seem so bad after all. Then Albert King showed up.

The man *was* his father and when he said something like "I've come to take you to Lexington to live, son." there was but no question that Riley would go.He'd leave his beloved cabin, Luther Henson's school and Reverend Fair's church behind. And the Elkhorn Jubilee Singers just had to be put on hold, for the time being.

So, by the time he moved to Lexington, a larger town about 60 miles to the west, Riley knew the rules of Jim Crow frontwards and backwards.

When Riley's father took him to Lexington, in Holmes County, he encountered a type of racism that was more pervasive. The Jim Crow rules in Lexington were strictly enforced. One of the first things his father did when they arrived there was point out a service station that had three doors, one said WHITE MEN, one said WHITE LADIES and the third said COLORED. That was the way it was in Lexington, only three counties to the west, in Holmes County. One Saturday afternoon Riley was running errands for his stepmother, delivering large baskets of clothes she had washed and ironed. When he neared the downtown section he saw a commotion; many people milling about the courthouse in seemingly a stage of excitement. Curious yet frightened, he was drawn to the scene. As he neared he saw that several white men were carrying a young man who was tied up with ropes. They hoisted the young black man upon a platform and hanged him. He, like many in the crowd, was sickened. Yet, no one, black or white, protested.

It made him angry, sad, and mad. He knew that it angered every black that was a witness to the awful event. But he also knew that it angered fair-minded white people. No matter, his shock and pain would stay with him.

He didn't like Lexington because of that tragedy and other reasons. He felt out of place. He was a country boy who'd attended a tiny country school. Now he was thrown into Ambrose Vocational High School, a public school with hundreds of children bussed in from all over Holmes County. He felt like what he was at the time, a country boy dressed in ragged clothing. He

The ruins of the Winfrey church. The cemetery is across the road and is still being used. Several generations of Oprah's ancestors served as ministers of the church which was on Winfrey-owned land. The family was well respected by their white neighbors

many of whom frequently attended services there, including members of the Palmertree, Hunt, Grice, Gibson families along with other neighbors. A spring down behind the church was said to have "fine tasting water." Friends were always welcome.

talked country and his manners were country boy manners. Many of the students at Ambrose wore clean shirts and nice trousers every day. And they spoke differently than he did; they spoke like educated white kids. Riley didn't know the rules and there was no one to teach him. He was soon in trouble with the principal, a short stocky man named Professor Seal, who shaved his head. "His solution to rule infraction (regardless of guilt or intent) was to have two burly football players hold the boy to be punished down across a wooden barrel and he'd whip the hell out of them," all the while speaking in a soft voice.

The lynching he'd witnessed caused Riley to wake up in the middle of the night with chills. He knew he'd never fit in at Ambrose. He didn't have the proper clothing, only his work clothes, and there was no one to ask how he could fit in there. His father knew no more about it than he did.

He was raised to be good and while the segregation of the Kilmichael hill country was in his blood, Lexington seemed to threaten him. Too, he felt he didn't fit in with the family of his father and Mama King, his stepbrother and three stepsisters. They even made him feel country. So, one "day in the early fall of 1938, he got on his bicycle and sped out of town, away from a school that seemed like a large, cold factory, away from a household where he'd never been explained the rules, away from feeling poor and shabby, and certainly away from a town that would display a dead body in front of the courthouse. He couldn't get away from there fast enough, failing to leave a note of explanation. The man that would one day sing his message to the entire world, left none for his father that day. He was just gone.

Did he realize it was some sixty miles of dirt roads to "Mr. Flake's farm?" The trip took two days. The first night he slept in a barn with some cows. By the next morning, however, his hunger was overpowering but he only had enough money to some spoke grease and a grape soda for himself. By late that afternoon he was fearful of passing out from the hunger. His legs ached and his head hurt and it was difficult for him to breathe, pedaling his bike up the endless hills between Lexington and Kilmichael.

It was late afternoon when he saw the old woman seated on her porch. She was staring at him. He stared back and, as if guided by an unseen hand, pushed his bike into her yard and explained that he was starving. She went into her house and brought him buttermilk and a big plate of bisquits.

Years later, when he'd become successful, he went back looking for the little old lady who fed him that hot day. The house was gone and no one could remember exactly who she was or what became of her.

He finally reached the Kilmichael area, half starved and exhausted. Must to his sorrow, Flake Cartledge had let someone else move into his cabin, not expecting him to return. It was about this time that he did live on the Henderson place for a few weeks but he was not there long

On January 15, 1940, a couple of month's after Riley left his father's house and returned to Kilmichael, his grandmother died. Next to his mother, Elnora Farr had been a source of strength and direction for him more so than anyone else in his life.

*(Note: *There is a question about how much was paid for this guitar. Even the buyer seems confused, as he has been quoted as saying he paid as little as $2.50 for it, all the way up to $15.00.*

A rural Mississippi version of a 7-11. Called the "rolling store" they hauled goods and groceries to remote farms out in the country to sell to housewives. They were especially popular in the southern part of Montgomery country which lacked paved roads.

Chapter Five

Working For The Man

AFRICAN AMERICAN novelist/essay-ist Ralph Ellison observed, "In the South. . .there were three general ways (for blacks to confront their destiny): They could accept the role created for them by the whites and perpetually resolve the resulting conflicts through the hope and emotional catharsis of Negro religion; they could repress their dislike of Jim Crow social relations while striving for a middle way of respectability, becoming, consciously, the accomplices of the whites in oppressing their brothers; or they could reject the sit-uation, adopt a criminal attitude, and carry on an unceasing psychological scrimmage with the whites, which often flared forth into physical violence."

The Famous St. John's Gospel Singers of Indianola, 1945. For Riley, they replaced the Elkhorn Jubilee Singers. Front row: Ben Carvin, John Matthew. Standing are Birkett Davis, O.L. Matthew and Riley King. Davis was also a member of the Elkhorn group.

Religion, its teachings, it camaraderie, its music were at the core of young Riley's life. Still, it was not the kind of religion that left him a slave looking skyward, alone, for salvation. He loved Gospel but. . .

There was another important dimension to Riley's musical and personal development. His association with "devil music," the dirty blues. Through the blues Riley rebelled against the system that kept his people oppressed, crippled by a life, no different in most respects than the horrible tradition that was slavery.

Whatever "otherworldly" narcotic that might have been present in Gospel music was offset by the razor sharp wit and emotional highs and lows found in the blues.

As B. B. King, Riley would explain that he lived through the worst days and years of racial oppression and poverty in Mississippi. "I was there," he said. "I know about it, so I sing about it. . . The blues was our way of communicating, and it's still my way of communicating. In other words, if you have me try to speak to people, I need my guitar, because then, I can hold their attention."

In the early days, though, B. B. and his group were making a reputation as a church rockin' Gospel group called "The Famous St. John Gospel Singers." Like Riley's early group, The Famous St. John Gospel Singers, gained a wide ranging popularity in the Delta region. They worked in all of the local churches, and, were even broadcast live on WGRM radio in Greenwood, and WJPR radio in Greenville.

It was a powerful music, this Gospel music. It not only rocked churches, it soothed, it raised spirits, it opened hearts. And its husky rhythms were directly related to an African past.

W.E.B. Du Bois observed that the slave songs that were the foundation for what would become Spiritual music as sung by the Fiske Jubilee singers and the more earthy Gospel music format were "the articulate message of the slave to the world. . . the message of an unhappy people, of the children of disappointment. . .The songs are indeed the siftings of centuries; the music is far more ancient than the words."

Long-time jazz singer Jon Hendricks once declared, "the language is music and rhythm the means of expression. That's where we brought it from. When we came here they outlawed the drum. It was our way of communication. It was rhythm. It was language."

Gospel music, as sung by Riley's group, had and always will have its primary foundation in and around the church. The music is designed to convey the essential message of the Christian faith, emphasizing the spirit of the Bible where, as in Job 38:7, "the morning stars sang together and all the sons of God shouted for joy."

The slave spiritual was the only music allowed on most slave plantations and consequently, it forms the major root on the tree of all black music. After the Civil War black music branched off into the more secular blues and an extended church music.

Blues music forms found much of their inspiration in the social conditions of the day. But it was church music that offered the only message providing a means of salvation from the depths of poverty and maltreatment. Often a promise for a better life after death, it seemed a better option than no better life at any time.

With the advent of the twentieth century Gospel music had developed into a mini-industry. Traveling church singers became more and more organized. Soon groups were traveling throughout the South, hired especially for church meetings or special events, both religious and secular.

Paul Robeson had for some decades been taking his "people's music" and sharing it with audiences around the world, including

Moscow. "I have sung my songs all over the world," said Robeson in the late 1930s, "and everyone found that some common bond makes the people of all lands take to Negro songs, as to their own."

African Americans like C. A. Tindley and Thomas Dorsey began writing and revamping the traditional religious music to such an extent as to create a new and vibrant genre of black sacred music.

Dorsey, considered the "father of Gospel music," confessed, "Blues is a part of me, the way I play the piano, the way I write. I was a Blues singer, and I carried that with me into the gospel songs."

Soon legends were born. There was Sallie Martin, Rosetta Thorpe, The Dixie Hummingbirds, Alex Bradford, Clara Ward and the "Queen" of them all, Mahalia Jackson. The musical "good news" quickly gained a wide audience of blacks and whites.

And, on a much, much smaller scale, there was Riley King and The Famous St. John Gospel Singers.

"The religion of the gospel songs," wrote Lawrence W. Levine (*Black Culture and Black Consciousness*), "remained a sustaining, encouraging, enveloping creed. Nevertheless, it differed markedly from the beliefs of the spirituals. Certainly it recognized and discussed the troubles, sorrows, and burdens of everyday existence but its immediate solutions tended to be a mixture of Christian faith and one variety or another of positive thinking."

Whereas the early spirituals were plaintive, Gospel was more a "joyful shout!" The religion called for movement, for action, for complete involvement of body and spirit and mind.

The world was in the bloody throes of World War II as Riley resettled in Indianola, Mississippi. That was 1943 and he turned eighteen, draft age.

There were haunting questions. No matter what the conditions at home, should young African American men and women fight and possibly die for a country that denied them basic human rights? If they fought, would racial conditions improve at home? Would their valor on the field of battle prove their right to be treated as equals in their homeland?

On December 7, 1941, the Japanese attacked the United States Naval fleet at Pearl Harbor, ushering the country into World War II.

Riley managed to avoid the draft and military service, though he spent some time in "uniform" at induction centers Camp Shelby, Hattiesburg, Mississippi and Fort Benning, Georgia. He spent much of his time entertaining fellow GIs with his still developing brand of the blues. But Riley's military career was to be very short.

On November 26, 1944, at age nineteen, Riley B. King took Martha Denton as his wife. The marriage and Riley's job in the agricultural industry earned him a military deferment. It was a bitter sweet blessing. The deferment required that he remain as a worker on the cotton plantation for the "duration of the war."

Riley toiled in the fields, played and sang Gospel in the churches, and played the dirty blues for nickels on street corners. The extra money helped but it still wasn't enough to break the cycle of poverty that would keep him sharecropping as had his father and his father's father.

His wife had a miscarriage, adding still another blue note to Riley's musical vocabulary.

Still, no matter the long unrewarding hours working another man's fields, he had dreams. Big dreams. Riley could never shake the pictures of great African Americans, singers, writers, preachers, politicians and teachers, who had become

Riley's marriage to Martha Denton and his job as a plantation worker got him a deferment from having to go into the army but it was something of a bittersweet victory. The Famous St. John's Gospel Singers weren't interested in spreading their fame too far

outside of Indianola. And fame and money was now what motivated Riley. He took up playing the "devil's music," the blues in local honky tonks such as this one in Itta Bena. His acceptance made him want more--which could only be found in Memphis.

"credits to the race." And, Luther Henson had told him more than once than he, too, could break away and make something of himself.

Riley's dreams didn't, a least to him, seem so grand in comparison to those fulfilled by the great black men and women about whom he had read. His dreams, he thought, were small in comparison. He wanted to play his guitar and sing. And he wanted to do it in Memphis.

Memphis, like Harlem, was to writers during the 1920s, the Mecca of the blues. It was where the music took shape. Where legends grew to heroic proportions. Memphis. It was there, only 120 miles to the north, yet, it was momentarily just out of reach.

But distances, seemingly short today because of advanced transportation, were great obstacles then. Blacks, especially, were forced to walk, most of the time, if they were to travel outside their immediate community. And, the north, for all its promises of hope and freedom, might as well have been millions, instead of hundreds or thousands of miles away.

Riley's efforts to encourage the members of The Famous St. John Gospel Singers to "take their act" on the road fell on the ears of the unconcerned. The five-man singing group, which included Riley's cousin Birkett Davis and John Matthews, was just not interested in the "risky" venture, given the conditions and the attitudes of the time period.

Unlike today, there was only a handful of black entertainers who were managing to make a living with their talent. The age of "race records" was in its fourth decade, and many, many more African American entertainers were receiving recording contracts. Still, there were no real guarantees.

Riley, alone, or with his Gospel group, had made great strides in the Delta area. In the local churches and juke joints, he was a hit. But how would his talent compare with the giants, those who lived and worked in Memphis, Tennessee. Up North!

Other than his short time at Camp Shelby and Fort Benning, Riley B. King had never left a football shaped area of central Mississippi, bounded on the west by the Mississippi Delta, and on the east by the red hills of the Kilmichael/French Camp area. But he had heard of Memphis. His cousin Bukka White, a blues singer and guitar player, lived in Memphis. Bukka introduced B..B. to the power of the electric guitar.

Riley knew that if he was to ever change

his life, change his economic status, he would have to leave the lush Delta, where cotton was king and men like Riley would always be in unrewarding serfdom to that king.

One day in May, 1946, Riley had had it. Martha, who had recently miscarried, moved in with her brother, leaving him little choice but to do the same. And then there were the German prisoners of war. The plantation owners treated them better than they did the blacks who worked there all the time. The Germans finished their day at 3 pm--but the hired hands such as B. B. were required to work until sundown or later.

One day B. B. forgot about the quirky tractor; it didn't always stop when turned off but would often do a post-ignition lunge. That day it did and the result was a disaster. As he watched helplessly, the tractor lunged backwards, smashed against the barn, broke off the smokestack and did hundreds of dollars worth of damage.

The rest of the day was a blur; at some point he went home and got his guitar. Before sundown he was out on Highway 49, headed for Memphis.

Of course Riley's cousin Bukka White was a star in Memphis. And the great Muddy Waters (right) had passed through there on his way from Indianola to find greatness in Chicago.

Chapter Six

Memphis

FOR ALL INTENTS and purposes twenty-one-year-old Riley B. King was broke and homeless when he arrived in the big city, Memphis, Tennessee. He had no immediate plans but knew that he had to find his cousin Bukka White (Booker T. Washington White) if he was to have any real chance of survival in the wide open town.

Riley didn't immediately locate cousin Bukka his first day in Memphis. There were too many people, far more than he had expected, although he had been expecting it to be crowded. He went into several places and asked for Bukka and while he was well

---

Riley B. King was twenty years of age when he left the plantation and his wife behind for his first assault on Memphis. But he soon found aspiring guitar players were a dime a dozen on Beale Street. And, there was that unfinished business in Indianola.

known just about everywhere, no one had seen him that day or knew where he lived, or so they told him. That night Riley slept in the back room of a saloon.

After a second day of searching, Riley found his cousin. He had a place to live. And cousin Bukka began Riley's serious study of the guitar.

Riley felt like a young gunslinger who seemed to meet his match or betters on every street corner. Musicians seemed to spring up from the sidewalks throughout Memphis, most especially on famed Beale Street, home of the blues.

But Riley wasn't prepared to return to the cotton fields in defeat. Bukka encouraged him and helped him with getting his guitar technique down. He hadn't expected that it would be easy. But he also hadn't expected as much quality competition, from other blues singers who were as hungry as he.

Memphis. It was big. Sprawling. Fast paced. And unmerciful. There was a hard edge to the men who haunted the Memphis streets. Many seemed lost. Hungry. Purposeless.

In the years between the Civil War and just after World War II, Beale Street in Memphis was the Main Street of Black Music, USA. It was Fifth Avenue and Rodeo

Drive and Bourbon Street all rolled into one, with a heavy flavor of smoked barbecue and a soul probing dose of the blues.

It was the home of the blues. And the nation's "murder capital."

The blues. Decent folks didn't listen to it, go to where it was moaned and groaned, or generally acknowledge it as anything other than the wails of the damned—souls damned because of their own sins. And, if the blues was the wails of the damned, Beale Street in Memphis was its fiery core.

One writer observed that "there were in Memphis about a dozen drugstores that made almost all of their profits by selling cocaine to Negroes and poor whites; at 5 cents and 10 cents a box."

But the man who would be proclaimed "Father of the Blues" was not born in Memphis, the Mecca. W.C. Handy was born on November 16, 1873, in Florence, Alabama, hard by the Tennessee River. His father and grandfather were both ministers which accounts for Handy's love of "Negro" spirituals.

Later in life, Handy would say over a radio broadcast in 1931, "Like tears, they were relief to aching hearts. . . these spirituals did more for our emancipation than all of the guns of the Civil War."

The statue of W. C. Handy facing Beale Street in Memphis. Called "The Father of the Blues" Handy actually was the man who "refined" the blues. Leader of a society band that played for white country clubs and such, Handy's band was spelled by a

group of locals at a white dance in Clarksdale, Mississippi. The crowd went wild over the local "blues" band, where they'd only offered polite applause to his group. That same night he heard a man play the slide guitar. And then the modern blues were born.

His love for spiritual music aside, Handy, over the angry objections of his parents, opted for a stage career. He joined Mahara's Minstrels in 1896 and performed coast to coast with the traveling group. His experiences from that point on became important research material for his blues.

"Behind the 'Memphis Blues,' 'St. Louis Blues,' 'Beale Street Blues,' 'Yellow Dog Blues' and others," explained Handy "were my personal experiences in rock quarries as a water boy. . . when I heard the labor songs of the steel drivers. . .Personal experiences in the mines, steel mills around Birmingham where I worked as a common laborer; three years residence in Mississippi, where I saw the aesthetic value in the songs of the cotton pickers, and as a traveling minstrel from coast to coast with the opportunity to observe that something within our group that takes us back to the shores of Africa from which we were transplanted, and that something was rhythm. . . With the American (Black) rhythm is paramount, intensified or diminished by his varying moods, and to express 'blues,' one disregards convention and uses the written note as only a guide, whether in blues or spirituals."

It has often been said (and written) that W. C. Handy was bilked out of his rights to his "Memphis Blues." And certainly a lot of black composers were victims of crooked music publishers, but W. C. Handy was not one of them. E. H. Crump, the "boss" of Memphis for over fifty years, paid Handy to write the music that became "Memphis Blues" as a campaign tune. The music helped Crump get elected and both he and Handy probably thought that was the end of it. However, there was a young man, barely in his twenties, who worked in the music department of Brys department store and who saw possibilities in "Memphis Blues" as sheet music, though it was different than anything that had ever been published before. He bought the publication rights to the tune for $250, a great deal of money in 1912. He then added the words that have come down over the decades with the tune. And of course he made a great deal of money from the Handy composed-for-hire Crump campaign song. Handy, however, had learned his lesson. He never sold all the rights to another song of his, and his next composition, "St. Louis Blues" was one of the most financial rewarding songs of all time. The great R&B singer Ruth Brown got a Grammy for her "Blues on Broadway" in 1991 and it, of course, included "The St. Louis Blues."

"St. Louis Blues" was an instant success.(In 1971 the story of W.C. Handy was
placed into the nation's Congressional
Record in an article written by Col. George
W. Lee. The article was actually read into
the record by Rep. James H. Quillen (R.
Tenn.). In his article Lee observed, "It was
Handy's great sense of values that caused
him to discover the nationalistic element in
the folk songs of black people in the back
country.")

Jelly Roll Morton's original arrangement of
"Jelly Roll Blues" was published in 1915,
becoming the first jazz arrangement to be
published in this country. Morton quickly
joined the ranks with other black composers
who were bilked out of their songs and
money by white publishers.

African Americans were making music in
the north and in the south. Though based
on the same rhythmic foundations, the
music in New Orleans, for example, was
somehow different from the music created in
the Memphis area. Still, it was all the blues.

Riley listened attentively to everything
cousin Bukka told him. Bukka was an
accomplished bluesman, a singer/guitarist
who had paid enough dues to become a char-
ter member of the moaning blues brigades.
After all, Bukka had done time behind the

walls and steel bars of the infamous Parchman Prison Farm in Mississippi. Its notoriety earned it a place in the blues as the "Parchman Farm Blues":

Judge give me life this mornin' down on Parchman Farm (sung twice)
I wouldn't hate it so bad, but I left
my wife and home.
I'm down on old Parchman Farm but I sho' wanna go back home. (twice)
But I hope some day I will overcome.

B. B. King biographer Charlie Sawyer describes Bukka, in his *The Arrival of B. B. King,* as "cocky, defiant, mischievous, charming in a rough sort of way, and delicate with his guitar. . ." And "Bukka possessed one quality that was indispensable to every bluesman: durability. Bukka was a survivor."

Riley would learn to become a "survivor," develop that durability that would allow him to tour year round, but it would take more time.He had much more to learn from Bukka.

The era of race records had allowed many more bluesmen to listen to and learn from the greatest players around. For Riley, Blind Lemon Jefferson, Lonnie Johnson, Charlie

Christian, Django Rhineheart and T-Bone Walker comprised a living "musical Bible" from which he religiously read.

From these men he learned as much about music as he did about life. "I lost my mother when I was nine," B. B. recalled in an interview, "so I could picture in my mind how Blind Lemon must have felt. . . a guy who had never seen anything as we see it. I thought so many times. . .of being around people and I didn't seem to fit. . .an outcast, always outside looking in."

Riley points to Lonnie Johnson as the performer who "linked him to jazz." Lonnie Johnson "had the respect of musicians," B. B. said, "but he also had the know how for mingling with the people. I like to think of myself as a Lonnie Johnson, a man without enemies.

And T-Bone's playing sold him on the instrument that would be his rhythmic voice, the electric guitar. "When I heard T-Bone Walker playing the blues on an electric guitar that just did it all. It was like I had become of age."

They would have an ongoing influence on Riley's playing.

"Every time that I feel the need for that charge in my battery again," B. B. explained in an interview, "I'll put one of them on. They seem to have one thing in common. The phrasing and—I call it shopping for notes."

His guitar playing improved dramatically under Bukka's guidance. Soon he could hold his own with the other "bluesman wannabes" that roamed Beale Street, played their moanful blues in Beale Park or just hung out in front of The W.C. Handy Club, or any of a couple of dozen others on Beale Street. But it wasn't enough. His music had not become a money-making career.

There were other thoughts troubling Riley as he tried to make himself heard as a bluesman in Memphis. He was an honest man and responsibilities back in Indianola troubled his sleep. He had left a wife in Indianola and a small financial debt to his ex-employer Johnson Barrett.

Riley decided to return to Indianola and take care of his debts. Making it as a musician in Memphis was still uppermost in his mind. But that could wait. At least for a time.

He would put in two crops for Barrett before finally settling his debts. He had not given up on his music over that period of time. And, most importantly, he had not given up his dream of making his music be heard among the giants on Beale Street.

It was late 1948 before Riley B. King,

After eight months in Memphis, living with, and taking lessons in both the guitar and life from his cousin Bukka White, Riley realized a couple of things. Guitar players of his experience were a dime a dozen down in Handy Park on Beale Street and he'd

left unfinished business back in Indianola, that included his wife Martha, and a financial debt to his ex-employer, Johnson Barrett. He decided to return and settle his debt by putting in two crops for Barrett. Two years later he was back on Beale Street.

wannabe bluesman, made preparations to return to Memphis. This time, he assured all who would listen, he would make it big.

Another important event was taking place in the closing months of 1948. It would prove to be one of the most important happenings in Riley King's life. WDIA AM radio switched to a black music format.

WDIA first went on the air in 1947, under the ownership of white owners Bert Ferguson and John R. Pepper. But the station was not successful until it went to a black format, featuring on-air personality Nat "Professor" Williams at the mike.

Chuck Scruggs, WDIA's first station manager, aimed its feeble 250 watt transmitter at the heart of the black community. The station quickly bonded with the community by passing out some 40,000 flyers, throughout the Memphis community, promising a station dedicated to servicing the black community.

All who heard Nat Williams' infectious laughter over WDIA were immediately hooked. He created shows that spoke directly to the community, like "Tan Town Jamboree," "Tan Town Coffee Club," and "Brown America Speaks."

There was a new, exciting sound in town. WDIA was deep blue and black. The infectious Nat Williams was soon joined on the air by other black jocks, including Rufus Thomas, Theo Wade, among others. And, shortly after its first months on air, a new voice, a real talent would join the on-air cast under the name "Beale Street Blues Boy" or the "Pepticon Boy."

When Riley B. King, guitar in tow, again arrived in the Memphis area, he felt he had real connections. He immediately sought out bluesman and radio jock Sonny Boy Williamson of KWEM radio in West Memphis, Arkansas, just across the river from the west end of Beale Street. His favor? Can I play a tune over the radio?

Sonny Boy opened his mike to Riley and asked his radio audience to call in and rate the young performer. Riley, though still some time away from being the polished performer he would become, got a number of calls, and a job.

The job was as a stand-in performer for the overbooked Sonny Boy Williams. The stand-in job at Miss Annie's Sixth Street Grill in West Memphis, though low-paying, was the beginning of Riley's career. He was offered a permanent job playing and singing at $25 per week. He had suddenly come a long way from the 35 cents a day he had earned working land owned by others.

Riley B. King wouldn't be called Riley much longer. When he made his second assault on Memphis, he had to cross over the bridge to get a start. The bridge led to West Memphis, Arkansas and radio station KWEM where blues man and radio jock, Sonny

Boy Williamson was the star. He dropped in to see Sonny Boy, asked to do a number on the air, and got enough response to land a job playing at Miss Annie's Sixth Street Grill. The pay wasn't much, $25 per week. More important, he was on his way.

The same day he landed the job for Miss Annie, Riley visited WDIA radio. After an unscheduled performance and an impromptu audience Riley King was offered a daily 10-minute radio show. The show, sponsored by a "tonic" known as Pepticon, was Riley's entree to a wider audience.

As the "Pepticon Boy," Riley was required to introduce the product with the "persuasive" little jiggle:

Pepticon, Pepticon, sure is good
You can get it anywhere in
your neighborhood.

For the remainder of the 10-minute Pepticon-sponsored show, Riley, live on-air, was allowed to play anything he wished. He let it all hang loose and his popularity soared.

Convinced that Riley King could gain a wider audience with a show of his own, WDIA station management hired Riley as a full-fledged DJ. He began hosting the "Sepia Swing Club" to eager blues lovers.

Another change had to be made to guarantee young Riley's continued radio success. All agreed that he had to change his name if he was to truly become the charismatic and memorable DJ who would bring even greater audiences to the station.

After much work, it was decided that Riley B. King would be re-christened "The Beale Street Blues Boy." The name was a real mouthful and was soon shortened; first to "Blues Boy King" and finally to the more memorable "B. B. King."

B. B. King's successful radio show earned him gigs at all the local blues joints. His reputation quickly spread throughout the South as WDIA radio cranked its wattage up to 50,000. Black radio was no longer a tiny voice whispered in the southern wilderness. It was now a full--bodied roar that could be clearly heard across a number of state lines.

Popularity aside, Memphis was still the South. "I still have fear somewhat, when I go home to Mississippi or to some of the other southern states," B. B. recalled for an interviewer for *The Black Collegian* magazine (1978), "where I wasn't allowed to go into the hotels and the restaurants. . .It was an unwritten law that you weren't supposed to go to this cafe, or hotel. You knew that if you wanted to live you just didn't go."

Yes, B. B. had gained some success, but he had yet to overcome the oppressive laws of his environment. And, he was not "free."

"There were water fountains in some places," B. B. recalls, "that said 'white' and 'colored.'"

The side effects of the oppressive laws and violence was a very real fear that added its bitterness to the developing blues. Says B. B., "That hidden fear still arises sometimes.

"It's like the old saying, you can take a guy out of the country but you can't take the country out of the guy. It takes a while for that to wear off."

It was part of life, of the blues that so beautifully, if painfully at times, recalled and expressed that life. Blues "is a feeling," B. B. told writer Mitchell Lansbery, "and it has to do with life—people living, doing well or not doing well, love affairs, togetherness or not togetherness. A guy always wishing, hoping things are going to be better. That to me is blues."

Still, B. B. had arrived. He was the envy of and embryonic hero to many young bluesmen wannabes. They followed B. B. to every club he played. They listened faithfully to his live radio broadcasts. B. B. was a long way from becoming enthroned as the "King of the Blues." But, his royal musical blood line was beginning to reveal itself in masterful blues. In 1949, B. B. King, radio jock and club singer, was suddenly offered an opportunity to record. It was the beginning of his historic recording career.

John Fair, the brother of the Reverend Archie Fair, the guitar playing preacher who was such a huge influence in the life of Riley (B. B.) King. "It was Archie's guitar but I'm the one who taught him the notes, how to get started playing it," said John.

Chapter Seven

"Three O'Clock Blues"

IT WAS AN IMPORTANT and exciting time for newly christened B. B. King. Things were happening very quickly as a diversity of career opportunities were offered him. It was time, he thought, to record.

B. B.'s first recordings were for Bullet Recording and Transcript Company. The small company was founded by Jim Bulleit. Bulleit had dabbled in race-records for some time, selling gospel records throughout the south. B. B. later recorded six singles for RPM Records.

The young blues singer was a major attraction on the local chitlin' circuit of

No one was around to capture that auspicious moment when B. B. King signed his first recording contract but we suspect he had a grin of happiness on his face that rivaled the one shown on the opposite page. The young B. B. was hot!

black clubs. He played nightly, beginning to show traces of the stamina and durability for which he would become famous.

B. B.'s popularity quickly crossed state lines. He played gigs in places throughout the tri-state area of Mississippi, Tennessee and Arkansas. He even returned home to Indianola, Mississippi, to prove to all who had doubted him that he had overcome. He was a star, if only in the tri-state area.

That anonymity would soon pass and B. B. King would suddenly become a household name among blues lovers, black and white, throughout the world.

But, shortly before B. B. King recorded the song that would rocket him into the spotlight, he was involved in a "mishap" that almost cost him his guitar. . .*and his life*.

B. B. was playing a gig in a little ramshackle club in Twist, Arkansas. It was one of hundreds of juke joints that dotted the tri-state area, providing much needed venues for blues performers.

Everything was routine until a fight broke out between two men. In the confusion someone knocked over the small kerosene stove that heated the joint. A fire erupted. The club cleared in seconds as customers and performers alike bolted for the exits.

To the surprise, more aptly, shock of all

present, B. B. King rushed back into the burning inferno. The crowd watched anxiously as the bluesman disappeared into the flaming structure. Frantic moments passed before B. B. King emerged from the building, clutching his *guitar* tightly to his chest.

The flames consumed the entire structure. A grim discovery was made in the smoldering debris, the bodies of two men. It was then that B. B. realized how reckless he had been. He had risked his life for a *thirty-dollar* guitar!

When he learned that the fight that started the fire was over a woman named "Lucille," B. B. named his guitar, "Lucille" as a constant reminder of his recklessness.

"I realized that I had run off without my guitar," B. B. recalled much later. "So I went back for it and when I did, the building, which was wooden, started falling in around me and I almost lost my life trying to save my guitar."

Though he never did get to meet the lady who triggered the furor, B. B. said, "I named my guitar Lucille to remind me never to do a silly thing like that again. "Cause I think you can always get another guitar, but you can't get another B .B. King."

Since that fateful and fiery moment, B .B. has owned a number of "Lucilles." Many

The young singer, newly signed to his first recording contract, was a smash hit in the tri-state area around Memphis, but he was still playing honky tonks where the sometimes unruly crowds didn't realize (or, in some cases, care) that they were witness

to the beginning of a major career, much less, the launching of a
genius. This photograph was taken in a typical juke joint, this
one in Clarksdale, Mississippi, by Marion Post Wolcott for the
Farm Security Administration. B. B. often played such audiences.

have been stolen or destroyed in automobile accidents, though he still treasures three of his original "Lucilles."

His original "Lucille" was a black Gibson guitar with a DeArmond pickup. He recalls that the guitar was half the length of the guitars he presently plays. He has since switched to a Fender model. And now plays a Gibson, semi-solid, thin-body guitar. "It's a good guitar," says B .B. "And it fits me. I'm a big guy. It lays right there real good."

(In B.B.'s honor, the Gibson guitar company produced B. B. King Standard and B. B. King Custom guitars for commercial consumption. Each of the black-bodied beauties sports the name "Lucille" on the head stock.)

But, it was not until 1951 that B. B. King got his real break in the business to which he would devote a great deal of his life. He recorded his seventh blues single, "Three O'Clock Blues" and the legend began.

"Three O'Clock Blues" was a hit. He made the coveted *Billboard* chart of hit records shortly after its release. The B. B.King single remained high on the chart and reached the number one spot in 1952. The single remained number one for 15 weeks.

Once B. B. gained national attention, offers to have him appear poured in from

B. B. and his guitar, Lucille. There have been dozens of Lucilles but the first one got the name after a woman named that almost cost him his life. Two men started a brawl over her and the honky tonk he was playing almost burned down around his ears.

venues across the country. He was about to embark on a whirl-wind tour of one-nighters that would last over four decades.

Immediately on the heels of B. B.'s chart-busting hit, United Artists booking agency in New York contacted him. The agency offered to sign B. B. to appear at Howard Theater in Washington, DC (on the campus of Howard University), the Royal Theater in Baltimore, and the famed Harlem showcase, the Apollo Theater.

B. B. could not believe what was happening to him. He was almost fresh from working the cotton fields. Thick, rough callouses still covered his hands. It had only been two years since he had left the plantation, determined that the separation would be permanent.

The Apollo Theater in New York had a longstanding reputation for showcasing the best performers available. It was a hold over from the fading years of the Harlem Renaissance. And, too, it was a testing ground for the best African American entertainers around.

The Apollo began as a white burlesque hall known as Hurtig and Seamon's Burlesque. But Harlem was in transition, from white to black as the writers of the Harlem Renaissance proclaimed the community the Mecca of Black Culture.

It was a time when black minds and culture were in full flower. It was a time of hot jazz and strutting blues, urban and rural, with white-only clubs like the Cotton Club providing an arena where Mayor Jimmy Walker, white actor/dancer George Raft and the wealthy Emily Vanderbilt could go and enjoy the talents of the likes of Bill Robinson, songstress Lena Horne, Ethel Waters, and musicians Duke Ellington and Cab Calloway.

But white ownership and patronage of Harlem clubs was not unusual. Neither was white ownership and black patronage of Harlem nightspots.

In 1934, Sidney Cohen purchased the burlesque theater and reopened it as the 125th Street Apollo Theater. The venue would specialize in black entertainment for black patrons. (Later, Frank Schiffman purchased the Apollo, and it would remain in his family until the 1970s.)

It was generally agreed that a black entertainer who had not performed in and "survived" the Harlem Apollo Theater had not yet arrived. All of the superstars of the world of black entertainment have, at one time or another, braved the demanding audiences that crowded the Apollo.

While many of the clubs had closed during the Depression, and remained closed, night life at the Apollo was very much alive. Some of the legends who stunned Apollo audiences include Ella Fitzgerald, Bessie Smith, Billie Holiday, Dinah Washington, Count Basie and too many more to mention. Though it would be a serious oversight not to mention Elvis Presley as an entertainer who conquered the famed Apollo.

When B. B. King stepped onto the stage at the Apollo Theater, he more than held the animated audience's attention. He survived and arrived as an important voice in the Black music world.

African Americans were making major strides, especially in the South, as B. B. began his series of tours, for the first time leaving the tri-state area of the South, his college, where he paid his dues and majored in his personal brand of blues.

B. B. King was making a brand of history of his own. On tour, he worked small clubs and bars in Memphis, Little Rock, Chicago, New York City, Jackson, Mississippi, Detroit, Michigan, and a number of clubs and concert dates on the West Coast.

"In 1956, I did 342 one-nighters," B. B. recalls. "So I took a break after that and

The Apollo Theater in New York had a longstanding reputation for show casing the best new performers available. It was the toughest audience a young performer could face but once B. B. King stepped on stage, he knew he had, at last, arrived.

Chapter Eight

On the Road

B. B. King and his funky blues had arrived. Always a hard worker, B. B., for the first time in his life, was truly making a living doing something he loved, playing and singing the blues.

His obsession with work, though, quickly took a toll on his marriage. B. B. and wife Martha divorced, leaving B. B. free to answer his calling to "spread the blues" to every corner of the world.

The popularity of B. B. and his band of bluesmen quickly increased. At last he was doing what he'd always dreamed of, even as the child who picked up Bukka White's guitar for the first time had his dream of fame.

B. B.King was, for the first time in his life, making a living doing something he loved, playing and singing the blues. But his obsession with work took a toll on his marriage, and he and Martha divorced, leaving B. B. free to travel and sing.

Engagements kept them working the tough southern "Chitlin' Circuit" of black nightspots on an almost daily basis. As soon B. B. and the band finished a gig in one place, they packed their gear and headed out onto the dark night highway bound for the next gig, a hundred or more miles down the dark, lonely highway.

Transportation was always a problem. There was no way that B. B. could transport himself and band from place to place by commercial bus or train. He was forced to buy a greyhound bus for the touring blues troup. He named it "Big Red."

Somehow B. B. found time from his all-consuming tour to slip into the studio to record. During the 1950s he recorded such classics as "Sweet Little Angel," "Eyesight to the Blind" and "Woke Up This Morning."

Other hits followed on recordings issued on the Crown and Kent labels from RPM. There was "Baby, You Lost Your Good Thing Now," "Five Long Years," "The Jungle," "Everyday I Have the Blues," "Did You Ever Love A Woman," "Crying Won't Help You" and "You Upset Me Baby."

The B. B. King brand of blues was in demand. His releases always sold at least 50,000 copies, including his best-selling LP, *B.B. King Sings Spirituals.*

Writer Phyl Garland (*The Sound of Soul*) described B.B.'s persona as "so gentle as to seem almost apologetic, his warmth and honesty such that he might be an old friend, even on an initial meeting."

On June 4, 1958, B. B. King remarried. His new bride was a beautiful young lady named Sue Carol Hall. They would remain together for almost a decade.

"Big Red" finally succumbed to the long road tours in 1958, after a crunching accident in Texas. B. B. had no choice but to purchase a brand new bus. He had engagements to fulfill and was determined to make them all.

For the most part B. B. King was playing and singing for all-black audiences. They crowded the small venues to hear the man who could express in beautiful music the agony they all experienced and shared. In the juke joints B. B. King never had to explain the blues. He was among family. They knew the blues, as intimately as an old friend.

B. B. once told an interviewer that "one of the reasons why a lot of the older blacks can relate to the lyrics, because they've had to go through it."

He asked the interviewer to "think of slavery, when the plantation owners split up families by selling some of them off and sending them away."

Then, B. B. explained, "Well, where I grew up, it wasn't exactly slavery as it was then, but these same kind of things happened. See my children never knew really that in the South you couldn't stay in hotels—and we're talking about in the late '50s and early '60s. How people would hang you; there were black men being castrated and murdered in many ways simply because they were trying to get rights. So they (children) all seem to laugh when you talk about it."

B. B. concluded, "Well, I lived through that. I was there, I know about it, so I sing about it."

But radio was the life blood of the recording artist. It was radio that introduced the widest audience to an artist's latest releases. It was through radio air play that new product was promoted.

Early in the 1960s, Top 40 radio turned its back on the man who was the self-styled blues Ambassador. Times and audiences had changed. The sizzling sixties, the Vietnam War and other social and political upheavals dictated new sounds, new emotions and directions, that many felt the dirty blues could not provide.

And, while there were a number of whites

who seemed to enjoy the blues, it was still black music, and even blacks seemed to turn their backs on the "devil songs." Somehow the funky, urban and country blues, reminded a growing number of African Americans of their less than regal roots.

The sixties were about radical change. The term "Negro" was no longer acceptable. It was replaced with Afro American by some blacks on the conservative flank, and more militant blacks opted for the term "Black." And with the name change to Black, followed the nation-rattling phrase "Black Power" from the lips of angry young black men and women, stubbornly sitting in and sitting down where they and their ancestors had historically been denied access.

For young blacks the blues was weak, whining, a throw-back to the submissive days of slavery and the sharecropper form of economic slavery that followed. For these young lions in revolutionary summer, the blues was a dirge sung only by defeated men.

But, these young people had little perspective on the blues. Too many of them, though well educated in the facts and rhetoric of so-called Black History, had never really learned anything about the blues and the duplicity which added more

Early in the 1960s, Top 40 radio turned its back on the man who was the "blues ambassador." Time and audiences had changed. The sizzling sixties, the Vietnam War and other upheavals dictated new sounds. A number of whites still enjoyed

the blues but blacks turned their back on the "devil songs" just as Memphis turned its back on Beale Street which had been going to pot throughout the decade. By the mid-sixties when it seemed B. B. was all washed up, so was Beale Street (above).

powerful and subversive meaning to the lyrics and the message.

"The blues is dying," B. B. croaked sadly. "It's being murdered by poor promotion. They hardly play it on the radio anymore. And when they do play it, it's at the wee early hours of the morning when very few people are up to listen to it."

The problem was simple, according to B. B. "When people don't hear it (the blues), they can't enjoy it. Older fans forget about it and younger people can't hear it to appreciate it in the first place."

He pointed out that "Black people don't teach the kids about Black blues singers. The blues singer hasn't been talked about. He hasn't been exposed as a person who's doing things which are worthwhile for a family to appreciate."

But there were more and more blacks, African Americans, who spoke out in opposition to the blues, a music that had no foundation in "black" culture. They were ashamed of the blues, a music which kept alive negative images of the past. Images best forgotten as African Americans, blacks, embarked on a new and upwardly mobile assault on the American Dream mountain in the sixties.

"Most of the people today," complained

B.B., "who know about the blues are people who were around when blues was played to and for people who weren't ashamed of the blues. These are the people who know about, respect, like and appreciate the blues. A small percentage of the kids of these people are aware of the blues because of their families who. . .weren't ashamed to speak out on it. Most of the new generation of people who were exposed to the blues at home haven't had a chance to be exposed to the blues, so they can't know about the blues."

It was a tragic misunderstanding. A misreading of a people's cultural artifacts.

B. B. was also disappointed by the general lack of respect given himself and his blues. "There's no reason why I can't sing the blues as a profession and be a gentleman," B. B. defended against charges that the blues were the moanful grumblings of drunken old black men, shiftless gamblers and worse.

"I would like to be given the same kind of respect for my style," B. B. pleaded, "that Sinatra gets for his."

The snub from both blacks and whites had a powerful impact on B. B. "I have always felt like a stepchild to some extent," B. B. told writer Jon Woodhouse. "The blues, my music, is a stepchild in popular music in

The Fourth Street Baptist Church at the corner of 4th and Beale was near Church Park, named after a prominent family. Nearby was the Solvent Savings Bank which was founded by Robert Church, Sr. The honky tonk row ran from the river but generally

stopped before it got to the church. There were and are several other large churches in the area, including a very large Catholic church attended mostly and historically by African American Catholics. There are, in fact, several Catholic schools in the city.

some ways. I'm still not making in a week what some people termed superstars make in a night. They can make it on eight concerts a year, and I'm out here 300 nights."

Dedication, durability and an obsession with his music made B. B. King a better performer. But somehow even the positive brought more blue notes into his world.

No, B. B. wanted to shout out to the world that "blues isn't just some sad music about a broken heart, a busted dream, or a painful love affair. Blues is much more than any of these things. . .it ain't nothing but living, laughing and loving."

B B. saw the blues as a very personal language with a very universal message to share. Why couldn't others see and feel they way he did?

Yes, "The blues is dying," B. B. croaked in the mid-sixties. But he never gave up the road. He never gave up his exhausting role as Blues Ambassador to the world. If the blues had taught him anything at all, he had learned that what some people call "patience" is much more, it is persistence and endurance under some of the worst conditions.

B. B. knew the blues would survive. It was an integral part of the fabric of the nation, of black people (even those who did not sing

Novelist Richard Wright, a fellow Mississippian, observed: "the most astonishing part of the blues is that, though replete with a sense of defeat and down-heartedness, they are not intrinsically pessimistic; (the music) is dialectically redeemed through...force."

the blues) and of American history, its present and its future.

"We black folk," wrote novelist Richard Wright, a fan of the blues, "our history and our present being, are a mirror of all the manifold experiences of America. What we want, what we represent, what we endure, is what America *is*. If we black folk perish, America will perish."

No. The blues was ill, but it would not die. It grew stronger from adversity, more bold, more sassy, more abrasive, in a word rebelliously revolutionary.

The blues is a resilient form and B. B. King was well aware of that. The blues, as described by Ralph Ellison, was indeed "an impulse to keep the painful details and episodes of a brutal experience alive in one's aching consciousness, to finger its jagged grain, and transcend it. . ."

The blues would survive, it was as durable as B. B. King.

In 1966, B. B. King separated from his second wife, explaining to a writer, "I think the main reason for us being separated was because of my traveling. . .music is my *life*; *blues* is B. B. King. Yes, I've been a crusader for it. . .(without the blues). . .I couldn't *live*!

"The blues," said Ralph Ellison, is "an impulse to keep the painful details and episodes of a brutal experience alive in one's aching consciousness to finger its jagged grain, and to transcend it...by squeezing from it a near-tragic, near-comic lyricism."

Chapter Nine

Back in the Blues

THEY NETWORKED THE SOUTH, B. B. King and his band of bluesmen. Like a band of nomadic Gypsies they seldom spent more than one evening in any city before moving on. Rare exceptions were the one-week gigs at places like the Howard Theater in Washington, D.C. and the Regal in Chicago.

They were plagued by flats, breakdowns, washed out roads, low pay and no pay. But they trudged on, weathering each storm until it was time to move on to make the next date.

In 1961 B. B. signed with ABC-Paramount but didn't cut his first noteworthy album

---

In a bout of urban renewal, the city fathers tore down much of Beale Street in the 1960-70s. Wiser minds sensed they might be destroying a good thing so the fronts of many buildings such as the one on the opposite page were given a new life for tourism.

until *B.B. King Live at the Regal.*

Interest in the blues continued to wane. B. B. persisted, and took his blues to anyone who wanted to hear them. He and his band appeared in places as far west as the California Hotel in Oakland, California and as far east as Harlem's Apollo Theater.

B. B. was still disappointed in the lack of recognition given himself and his band. Where was the R-E-S-P-E-C-T?!

"Now, I'm not saying that blues is supposed to be praised so much over everything else," B. B. would say, adding, "but I think it should be respected."

Respect. Recognition. Denied to the blues as they were denied to millions of African Americans, resulted in the creation of further blues. It seemed a vicious cycle of blues creating blues.

But the declaration that the blues was dying or dead was premature. B. B. was playing the blues. Determined not to let anyone forget. And aging bluesman Muddy Waters rasped, "I ain't worried about the blues gonna die. You're always gonna have some blues out there. Can't everybody live on top of the ship."

B. B. struggled on, saying "For us (blacks) the blues is almost sacred. To quit at this point would be letting down those fans who have stayed with me all these years."

He knew he had to change. The blues couldn't remain the same and stay alive. "One thing I've had to keep in mind," B. B. says, "even though you keep the basics and your identity intact, you do have to change a bit with the time because if you don't, the world passes you by. . .I like to think of myself kind of like the roach! He adapts to whatever the situation. He's been around since prehistoric times, so he's still there and ready to move when the lights come on."

There were others listening to B.B.'s blues. They were not of the Delta. They were not traditional blues lovers. They were not black! But they listened to this raucous music, from as far away as England. They listened. They learned. They copied. And they profited by the unauthorized collaboration with the man who would be King of the Blues.

"I was so very hurt that my singin' or playin' was just a *job* for me," confessed B. B. "I *really* hurt, believe me. I've had many people to ask me if I were bitter because a lot of white kids and other people would play things I had would make a lot of money, but I wasn't bitter. I was just *hurt*, because I thought that if these people thought enough of me to play like me and to do the

Bobby Bland and B. B. have been friends for over fifty years. King was already on Beale Street about a year when Bobby showed up and immediately became B. B.'s "favorite blues singer. Bobby can sing anything but he gives the blues with

that gorgeous satin voice of his, something it never had before. Whe he signed with my label, ABC, I got to do something that I'd dreamed of doing ever since I met Bobby. I wasn't in his category as a vocalist, I wanted to record with Bobby. ABC let us."

things that I was doin', why couldn't they give the original a chance?"

B.B.'s big chance came in the mid-sixties. A major white band had stepped forward to admit the impact music by B. B. King and other bluesmen had on their own work. Though B. B. had been playing his blues professionally for more than twenty years, he was suddenly "discovered," when whites recognized his existence and gave credence to his body of work.

B. B. recalls "when the white kids found out that groups like the Rolling Stones and other rock groups that they idolized, were using blues in their arrangements, they had to do research on us. They re-imported our sound."

With the research and re-importation of the blues came long over-due recognition for B. B. King. In 1966 B. B. performed at the famed Fillmore Auditorium in San Francisco, before a majority white audience. He received a standing ovation from the sold-out crowd. And, he again was honored with a standing ovation after his performance at the Cafe Au Go Go in New York City.

B. B. King and his brand of blues was in the process of crossing over, reaching beyond the limiting "race music" label and winning over new, non-black fans. But too often crossing over meant crossing out some of the raw edges of the deep blue-black-blue blues. Would B. B. compromise himself? His music? His voice to express his history?

"The blues is dying as we know it," B. B. says. "I am one of the few remaining blues artists who people feel still sings and plays the blues well. It's something I feel is worthwhile."

It was a curious proposition at best. B. B. had not changed. His music had not changed. Yet, as his black audience molted away like feathery dandruff, he was slowly gaining an avid audience of energetic young whites. What could they possibly know about the blues?

Critics took notice. Their potentially poisonous pens were kind to B.B., with one critic celebrating King "as one of the best guitarists of his time."

Another critic would observe that King had "a magnificently casual stage presence—loose, easy, beautifully timed and always in complete control of his performance and his audience."

B. B. and his bluesmen were also beginning to get gigs in venues far removed from the "chitlin circuit" of juke joints and ramshackle halls. In 1967, B. B. brought the

Backstage following a concert on March 11, 1989. Sid
Seidenberg (B. B.'s manger and friend, who has skillfully put a
much larger career together for the blues singer than anyone
thought possible.) Flanking B. B. are U-2's Bono and The Edge.

B. B. opened the U-2 concert in Fort Worth, Texas, the following year at their request. Bono had written a song for him and B. B. to sing in duet at Fort Worth. The song was "When Love Comes to Town" as the crowd cheered. It was a high for B. B.

good news blues to the prestigious Montreux Jazz Festival. A portion of the performance was aired over PBS-TV.

In 1968, B. B. was invited to perform at the Newport Folk Festival. In 1969, he rocked the Newport Jazz Festival and the Texas International Pop Festival.

The Rolling Stones was the next to shine a real spotlight on the bluesman when the group asked B. B. to go on an eighteen city European tour. The Stones were anxious to introduce the blues giant they adored and copied to their white rock fans. The introduction was explosive. The blues had found an eager audience.

Television appearances quickly followed, including the first of what would become numerous appearances on the super hot Johnny Carson "The Tonight Show." He also was a guest on the Mike Douglas Show, the David Frost Show and the Merv Griffin Show.

B. B. King's easy manner, impeccable attire and magical blues combined to make him a hit at each appearance.

"Until the days of rock and roll," B. B. once told a reporter, "a lot of places just wouldn't accept us. People like Mike Bloomfield, Elvis Presley, the Beatles and Fats Domino, helped us out."

It seemed that B. B. and his blues had truly arrived, shaken off the dust of anonymity and actually stepped under the spotlight and before the camera's eye. But B. B. knew differently. No matter his sudden success and acceptance. He was still an African American, a black man, living in the white man's South.

In 1969, B. B. explained to writer Phyl Garland the reason he could not move into one of the units in a Memphis apartment building he had recently purchased. "New Memphis, as you know, is not completely integrated," B. B. said. "So I bought this building in a white area. The lady that sold it to me was white and she knew she was selling it to a Black man, but she knew who I was. But I can't *live* in my apartment building because if I do, I'm likely to lose my tenants there."

The blues was definitely alive and well. By the closing months of the sixties B. B. King had toured the United States and Europe. He had also appeared in some of the most prestigious clubs in the world. But he was still troubled.

Where were the new singers of the blues? The young lions' whose moanful growls would replace B. B. Who would become the new blues king when B. B. decided to abdi-

B. B. meets the Rolling Stones. Keith Richards and Mick Jagger
were scholars of black music and felt that blues men deserved a
wider audience. Through "sheer conviction" they helped to introduce that audience to B. B. King, by inviting him to open a

tour for them. He told Guitar magazine that he was gland he was
opening and not following the Stones who were enjoying such
hits as "Honky Tonk Woman," "Ruby Tuesday" and "Jumpin'
Jack Flash." "That's what the hard core rockers were there for."

cate his throne?

"Only very rarely," B. B. says sourly, "do young artists come up to me now asking for help to become a blues singer. And, as I look around me, I really don't see that many real hardcore prospects."

He could only dream of the early days. Long hot days in Memphis where the blues was concocted like some magical potion. "It was segregated then, so white and black couldn't just go and sit in some place and play," he recalls. "We would sneak up to a club and there we would play. . . and learn from each other. . .and be friends.

And the young blues wannabes, their shoes thin, their faces eager, the message blue, would, "in the evening . . leave their job and come and congregate at the Beale Street park and that's where you trade ideas."

But, then, in the closing days of the sixties, it hurt B. B. that he was being ignored by African American colleges. Only one, Albany State in Georgia, reportedly asked B. B. to perform his blues.

"The blues is often seen as an Uncle Tom expression," explains historian Hamilton Bims, "a cowardly admission of impotence and despair; while the projections of the James Brown school are viewed as infinitely more consistent with the current black mood."

"I'm disappointed," B. B. admitted in an interview, "that my people don't appreciate me like the whites."

Chapter Ten

The King's Reign

1 970 was a very good year for bluesman B. B. King. He premiered in Las Vegas at Caesar's Palace and appeared on the highly popular, "Ed Sullivan Show."

As importantly, B. B. was finding time to get into the studio to record albums hungry fans craved. In 1968, signed to the Bluesway label, B. B. cut the album *Blues On Top of Blues,* which featured the single "Paying the Cost to be the Boss," which made the music charts.

But it was in 1970, that B. B. would record the song that would become his trademark over all others. The tune, "The Thrill Is Gone" from the 1969 LP *Completely Well,*

Kingman Brewster, the president of Yale presents an Honorary Doctor of Music from Yale University to Dr. Riley B. King. B. B. has also been similarly honored by Tougaloo College, Rhodes, Berk College of Music, and the University of Mississippi.

had an immediate impact on the music charts.

His 1969 *Live and Well* LP prompted Downbeat magazine critic James Powell to call the LP ". . .the most important blues recording in many years. For the first time, B. B. was allowed complete freedom to develop his own format. . .the singing is right on!"

Guitar Player magazine named B. B. the "world's top blues guitarist" in early 1970, referring to King's style as both innovative and complex.

The world opened her arms to B. B. King and his blues.

On November 23, 1973, B. B. King joined with Sly & The Family Stone for a televised concert. It was a major step forward, linking the blues great with the innovative Sly.

B.B.'s "I Like to Live the Love," hit at #13 on the Soul Brothers Top 20 of March 21, 1974. And in May B. B. made another appearance at Harlem's Apollo Theater. He performed in a special concert for Harlem's young people and then rapped about the blues.

In October of 1974, B. B. joined bluesman John Lee Hooker and violinist Papa John Creach on "Midnight Special," a late night television variety show.

In the early '70s B. B. became a world traveler touring in Africa twice, under the auspices of the United States State Department. He took his much appreciated blues to Ghana, Lagos, Chad and Liberia on one tour. And on his second African tour, in 1974, B. B. performed in Zaire for the Muhammad Ali vs George Foreman fight.

In 1978, again at the request of the State Department, B. B. performed in another country, Mexico, this time. He and his band were representing the United States at the International World Cultural Festival. They were among 200 artists from around the world to be so honored.

B. B. also won the blues category at the 11th Annual NAACP Image Awards.

And, in 1979, B. B. became "one of the first American contemporary musicians to tour Russia in cooperation with the United States State Department and the Soviet Cultural Exchange."

"We gripe a lot," B. B. said after his trip to Russia, "about problems we have over here—America—like prejudice. Well I didn't notice any prejudice while I was over in Russia. But I didn't notice but 13 blacks while I was there. Three of those worked for the U.S. government in the Embassy over there and the other 10 were African

For several years now it has been hard to pick up a copy of Blues Guitar Player magazine without reading something about Bonnie Raitt. Among her admirers are B. B. King "Best damn slide guitar player working today" for whom she was opening

act on several tours a few years back; John Lee Hooker who says: "nobody gave B. R. nothin'. She earned it, just like B. B. earned his." Another big mutual admiration society is between Bonnie Raitt and Ruth Brown who frequently tour together.

exchange students."

Though quickly becoming a world figure, B. B. had not forgotten the humble roots from which he sprang. In 1971, he began devoting as much free time as he could spare to providing free concerts for inmates in correctional institutions and prisons across the country. He could not forget that the very blues he sang sprang from the experiences of men like the ones before him in Cook County Jail, and the other institutions he visited.

As he searched their faces, B. B. could not help but wonder if one of the prisoners might rise to become a Bukka White, a Leadbelly, or a B. B. King. The LP *B. B. Live At The Cook County Jail* was a bold experiment that began a twenty--year commitment to performing in the nation's prisons.

Included on the "Cook County Jail" LP were the hit single "The Thrill Is Gone," "Sweet 16," and his first hit, "Three O'Clock Blues."

In some 20 years, B. B. would perform for inmates in over 60 correctional institutions, including prisons in Virginia, Miami, Florida, New York City, and Columbus, Ohio. He would become somewhat of an expert on inmate problems though it had not been his intention.

He spoke out on behalf of prisoners. "I think something should be done about speeding up trial dates," B. B. explained to all who would listen. "It's pretty bad if a guy isn't convicted for one thing but has to stay in jail because he can't raise enough bail money."

In 1971, B.B., along with attorney F. Lee Bailey, co-founded Foundation For The Advancement Of Inmate Recreation & Rehabilitation, or F.A.I.R.R.). "A lot of my boyhood friends ended up in prison," B. B. explained, "and it was only by the grace of God I didn't end up there myself. Prisoners are human beings and people first. By bringing outside entertainers and people in, the prisoners know that outsiders care. We hope that gives them a ray of inspiration."

King also promised "to see to it that prisoners get instruments, a lot of them have asked for them, books and other recreational and educational materials."

On May 2, 1970, B. B. King debuted his all-blues show in famed Carnegie Hall. It was a sign that the blues had been accepted by a white audience of blues lovers.

And in 1970 he won a coveted Grammy Award, the first of many, for his hit single, "The Thrill Is Gone." The award was in the category, Best Rhythm & Blues Vocal

Ruth Brown and B. B. King are flanked by executives of the Philip Morris Company who sponsored a concert at Carnegie Hall in January, 1994, to kick off a tour of Europe, which ended up at the New Orleans jazz festival where B. B., Aretha

Franklin and Ruth all headlined a show. Only four nights before the Carnegie Hall appearance, Ruth's new condo in Sherman Oaks, California had been completely destroyed by the Northridge earthquake. Her dog was killed in the wreckage.

Performance, Male.

He was a regular on the college circuit and at the jazz and blues festivals throughout the world. And, in 1973, he received his first of a series of college honorary degrees. The first was an L.HD from Tougaloo College in his home state of Mississippi. Yale University presented B. B. with an Honorary Doctorate of Music in 1977; Berklee College Of Music honored B. B. with a Doctorate of Music degree in 1982, and Rhodes College of Memphis presented him with an honorary Doctorate of Fine Arts in 1990.

After receiving his Honorary Doctoral degree from Yale, B. B. quipped, "I felt like maybe I was cheating a little bit. Here these students have worked four years for their degrees and I (got there that day and) was getting an honorary one."

In 1983, B. B. King felt he had come full circle. He returned to Indianola, Mississippi, not a failure, but a wealthy world traveler. He came home, where he had labored "sun to sun" for as little as 35 cents a day.

B. B. was 57 years old. It had been almost four decades since he turned his back on the cotton plantation. Had things changed any?

It was a gala event. The press came from

around the world, anxious to witness the homecoming of the King of the Blues.

"For the first time in my life," said King on that special day in June of 1983, "I don't feel like I'm the prodigal son anymore. I feel like I'm home."

A party was given, with 125 leading whites and an equal number of black community leaders in attendance. It was the first time these community leaders from both races had "mingled" together on a social basis. It was a magic moment.

It was ironic. Dr. King had marched, prayed and died, there in the South. For the cause of brotherhood and freedom. But little had changed in the little community of Indianola, Mississippi.

Little had changed until a one-time sharecropper, now wearing an expensive three-piece suit and flashy diamond rings and toting an expensive electric guitar, came home as a hero.

A man who had been afflicted with the blues young. But he found a way to cope with the blues, to learn from the blues and to transcend and profit from the blues.

The two-lane street that fronted Gentry High School was renamed B. B. King Road in the bluesman's honor. A festival and concert was also staged. For B. B. it was a proud moment. Not so much because of the recognition, but because of the brotherhood that seemed to bond the races for the first time in his life.

"These people grew up in a segregated society, like me," B. B. explained to a reporter present. "And I'm sure that even when people of good will wanted to do something to help change things, pressure from their families, their business associates and so on, made that very difficult for them to do."

Yes, it was indeed a very special moment for B. B., who said, "I've been back to Indianola a number of times, last night, being able to shake hands with the elite of Indianola on a social basis, well, that was my real homecoming."

Later, B. B. and Charles Evers, brother of slain civil rights worker Medgar Evers, drove to infamous Mississippi State Prison at Parchman. There B. B. gave a free concert for some 2,000 inmates.

"There are so many underprivileged kids in here," Evers told the captive audience. "Not blacks, not whites, kids. . ." B. B. isn't just bringing the blues to these people, he's bringing them good will, and inspiration. And he's letting all of Mississippi know how important he is as an ambassador of good will for the state—and for the entire country.

Though a portion of Mississippians seemed to be finding common ground, the fiery Reverend Jesse Jackson was pointing to the state's major faults.

"We found new forms of voter denial in Mississippi," Jackson declared in Washington, after a tour of the southern state. "They no longer use the poll tax, the property tax, literacy tests of terror at the ballot box. The new tools are gerrymandering, annexation, at-large elections, single-shot balloting, primary runoffs and dual registration."

In 1984, B. B. King was inducted into the Blues Hall of Fame. In 1986, he was inducted into the Rock 'N Roll Hall Of Fame, honoring his influence on rock artists like Eric Clapton and Mike Bloomfield.

Also in 1986, B. B. and his band were honored for their college performances with the National Association for Campus Activities Hall Of Fame Award.

"White kids," B. B. said, "especially on the college campuses, are some of the greatest audiences to have. I wish that we could get black youth and the older whites into our music. Then I would feel that I have brought about a balance as an artist. I guess it goes way back that middle-class blacks looked down upon the blues and they've passed it on to their children. They just don't want to identify with it as part of their heritage and culture."

Performance Awards Polls voted B. B. Blues Act Of The Year in 1985, 1987 and 1988.

B. B. received the Grammy "Lifetime Achievement Award" in December of 1987 at the first Grammy show ever televised. And, in 1990, he was presented the "Lifetime Achievement Award" from the Songwriter's Hall Of Fame.

In 1989, B. B. went on tour as a special guest of the rock group U2. He was also featured on U2's *Rattle and Hum* album, in "When Love Comes To Town."

B. B. continued to receive special honors in the 1990s. He was among sixteen American citizens to receive the tenth annual National Heritage Fellowship on September 26, 1991. It is the "highest honor the United States Government can bestow upon a traditional artist."

It was B.B.'s second such honor from the United States Government. On September 10, 1990, he was honored with a Presidential Arts Medal by President George Bush at an impressive White House

Ceremony.

On February 19, 1991, the first Orville H. Gibson Lifetime Achievement Award was presented to B.B at a ceremony at the Hard Rock Cafe in New York City.

On February 20, B. B. won his fifth Grammy Award, taking the Best Traditional Blues Recording category. Since 1969, B. B. has received fifteen Grammy Awards nominations.

In late 1991, B. B. took advantage of modern video technology and performed on a three part instructional video series. Structured like a documentary, the videos featured B. B. King and his band in performance, as well as candid comments from B. B. on his major musical influences and his experiences over a 40 year career. The videos were made available through DCI Music Video.

But B. B. has a unique style, one that cannot be duplicated. "When I sing," B. B. explains, "I play in my mind; the minute I stop singing orally, I start to sing by playing Lucille."

And, he has a special way of closing his eyes tightly while he interprets the blues lyrics that have made him famous. "When I'm singing," B. B. explains, "I see the person in my mind whom I'm singing about. If something clouds my memory while I'm singing—lets say somebody in the band laughs—I can still sing. But it's not real anymore. The spell is broken."

B. B. continues to weave a magic spell with his blues, crusading to make certain the blues are properly presented and perceived.

"Some folks think if you're a blues singer," B. B. says, "you've got to be a guy sitting on a stool looking North, with a cap on your head facing South, a cigarette barely hanging in your mouth to the East, and a jug of whiskey sitting next to you on the West."

It's a stereotype B. B. has challenged at every opportunity. He is always the polished gentleman, prepared to take his blues and "dress 'em up to sell."

B. B. recognizes the importance of being timely with his music, without distorting it, changing it into something never intended. "Times change," he says, knowingly. "People change. It's young people's time. And if I have to include a little soul and jazz to get some more Blacks into the blues, you can believe I'm going to do just that. But, then again, I've never pretended to be pure. Critics want to freeze me in time. I refuse to let that happen."

In Memphis, in September, 1995, B. B.

celebrated his seventieth birthday. Actually the celebrating started back at the first of June, with a special appearance in Indianola.

He has been playing and singing either Gospel or blues his entire life. It seems that it would be time for him to settle down, to take a break from the tour circuit. No way. B. B. continues to tour the world, playing a gig in Japan, Australia, New Zealand, France, Spain, Germany, Mexico and a score more. The world is his stage and upon it he continues to sing the blues.

Is it time to quit?

No! says B. B. Though he has slowed down a great deal from the break-neck pace of more than 270 gigs a year. "I don't have to work as hard as I do," says B. B. "But I couldn't have stopped before, even for a short while, as some of my ladies pleaded for me to do. If I had the blues would no longer be alive. I hope my kids will forgive me. I hope they understand why I was never there."

B. B. has, over his lengthy career, recorded more than 90 albums. He has recorded with some of the greatest entertainers in the history of blues *and* rock.

The King of the Blues continues to work. It is important to him. And as he looks back over his illustrious career, the awards and honors he received, there is only on thing of which B. B. is truly proud.

"The little talent I had," says B. B., "led me to better my condition, not only that, but to keep twenty-five people on my payroll working, twenty-five people that are paid and take care of their families from this one black blues singer. And I'm very *proud* of

PHOTO CREDITS

Tempe Woods, Kilmichael, Mississippi: 22, 25, 30-31, 38-39, 41, 42, 45, 48-49, 52-53, 64, 67, 75, 78-79, 89, 98-99, 125. Ray Locke: 70-71, 84-85, 108-109, 120-121, 144-145, 148-149, 154. Library of Congress: 57, 151. MCA 126, 133, 138. MCA/ Daniel Root: 182-183. MCA/Chess Files: 13, 103. MCA/ Lester Cohen: 166-167 The Center for Southern Folklore/William Ferris: 170. Dorothea Lange/Farm Security Administration: 27, 116-117. Marion Post Wolcott/FSA: 130-131. Gibson Guitar: 21. SAS/INC: 162-163. Philip Morris Company 178-179. Players International Photographs: 8, 15, 137, 158-159 Far Out Productions: 17.